OSPREY POINT

David Reinhart

Cardinal
Press

To Christine, with love.

CHAPTER 1

THE SUN WAS NOT EVEN A glimmer in the eastern sky, even though the dashboard clock of the red Ford Ranger pickup said it was after six. Dawn in New England came very late in January. In the headlight beams, dirty snow appeared along the shoulder of the narrow road. There was no traffic to draw the driver's attention away from the possibility of ice on the black pavement.

Barely visible in the dim glow of the dashboard lights, the driver was a bulky giant of a man wrapped thickly against the cold.

A flashing yellow light ahead marked his turning place. The truck slowed and made a left onto what was, to all appearances, a four-lane highway leading away from the two-lane secondary road. After the turn, an orange glow could be seen in the distance. It was in the east, but not the color of sunrise, and it seemed wrapped in mist while the skies above were filled with sharp winter stars.

A guard shack at the intersection contained two people whose heavy clothing made them into walking barrels. They barely gave the truck a glance as it passed their post. It was almost the end of their shift, and they were tired and very cold.

The driver continued down the long access road, coming to a huge parking lot filled with hundreds of cars. As he drove, the eerie glow in the sky grew brighter and the mist became more definite, swirling around in the light. Tall stacks appeared through the bare trees and massive buildings, everything surrounded by a double fence topped with barbed wire. Now you could tell that the orange glow came from dozens of sodium streetlamps scattered over the flat land.

Near a long corrugated steel building, two stories high, was an entrance to the lot. The man turned in and then started driving back in the direction he had come. Moving in starts and stops, it quickly became obvious that he was looking for a parking place as close to the building as he could get. He was not very successful in his search, finally finding an empty spot more than two blocks from the building. It was going to be a long, cold walk.

He parked and then turned off the lights and the ignition. Opening the door, he squeezed out of the truck onto the unpaved frozen earth, locked the door, and placed the keys in his jacket pocket. Turning, he bent his head to the wind coming from Long Island Sound and started walking quickly to the building.

As he approached, the lights revealed more details. The man was not too tall and glasses glinted on his face. There was a mustache showing above a white scarf, with a suggestion of a beard underneath. He reached the building where a sign above the door proclaimed MAIN ACCESS POINT. He pushed it open and stepped inside.

The change from frigid cold to normal warmth felt like walking into a sauna. The heat and bright fluorescent lights stopped him for a moment. He stood at the entrance of a huge room, catching his breath.

Away on his right was a counter, behind which stood several uniformed guards. In back of them were hundreds of pigeonholes, the letters of the alphabet running above the top row. *Pigeonhole* was a very apt name for the little spaces because the whole assemblage was enclosed in steel fencing, making it a veritable pigeon loft.

The man walked toward the counter, pulling down his scarf, confirming the existence of a beard, a very red one. Reaching the counter, he called out, not to any guard in particular, "Badge number C2092, please."

One of the guards, this one a short and pretty blonde with what looked like a .357 Magnum hanging from her belt, went over to the column marked with an "C," ran her hand down the column, checking the contents of each hole. Finding the right number, she turned to the man, compared his face with the picture on the badge, and asked, "Name?"

The man answered, "Strong, Alex."

Satisfied, she slid the badge to him through an opening in the cage.

The man named Alex picked it up, fumbling for a key-shaped piece of blue plastic hiding behind the badge. He turned toward what looked for all the world like security checkpoints at an airport concourse. There were five of them, but only two were working now. He walked toward the moving belt of an X-ray machine, pulling his keys out of his pocket, along with a very large Leatherman tool from a pouch on his belt, and placed them in a plastic bowl. He stepped through the frame of the metal detector, paused to pick up his belongings, and then moved to another metal doorframe just beyond. This machine was also found in some US airports. Its job was to sniff out the telltale odors of explosives.

There was one more barrier to pass: a stainless-steel turnstile that went from floor to ceiling. Slipping the blue plastic key into a box with green and red lights, Alex waited for the light to turn green and a loud *thunk*. Somewhere in the building, the master security computer read the code embedded in the key. It looked up the code in a table containing about ten thousand entries. It verified that the holder of this key was privileged to enter this site at this time then unlocked the gate. If the red light had lit, he would have been surrounded by armed guards before he could scream, "Don't shoot!" He'd seen it happen once, thankfully to somebody else.

Pushing the revolving bars around, Alex reached what looked like a regular glass door, but the polycarbonate it was glazed with could stop a bullet from an AK-47. Pausing only a moment to pull up the scarf, he pushed his way out. He was now inside Osprey Point Nuclear Generating Station, the largest atomic power plant in the world.

Even though Alex was now inside the fence, he still faced another quarter-mile walk to his office on the far side of the complex. Unlike the utility company gentry, the offices of the maintenance contractor, Alex's employer, were neither convenient nor comfortable. With the wind whipping in from Long Island Sound, just getting to work was a major accomplishment on some winter mornings.

His path took him past an immense cube of concrete. Just as he reached the center of one wall, there was an incredible *whoosh* of noise above him, a blast like a hundred steam engine whistles but much lower in pitch.

First, he jumped, and then he realized what was happening. *Damn! They're blowing the steam on Unit III again! I wonder what's gone wrong now ...*

In the ten minutes it took to reach the old mobile-home "temporary" building, his feet and fingers were freezing. Outside the building was the time shack, literally a small shack manned by only one timekeeper this time of day. Behind the young lady at the window were hundreds of hooks, each intended to hold a small brass disk with a hole punched in it. Most of them were empty already since the actual construction workers got in before Alex.

"Hi, Peggy," said Alex. "Got the heater going in there? Let me have number 221, please."

The timekeeper gave him a tired smile, turned around, grabbed his tag, and passed it to him.

This ritual was an ancient part of the construction trade. Every day, every worker "brassed in" at the start of shift and "brassed out" at the end. It went back to the days when few workers were literate and gave a quick way to verify who was missing should an accident happen on the job site.

Alex took the disk and then ran up the wooden stairs and into one big room crowded with desks. Under glaring fluorescent tubes, men in work clothes and hardhats sat talking on telephones, talking with each other, and poring over documents and drawings. Right now, because of the steam release from the generator building of Unit III, there was even more activity than usual for shift change.

The steam posed no harm. It was from the "cold" or nonradioactive side of the heat exchanger attached to the reactor core. When things were working right, the steam would spin a turbine turning two turbo generators capable of producing 1,154 megawatts of electricity. Right now, due to some malfunction in equipment or flaw in instrumentation, that super-hot water was making very expensive puffy, white clouds over Connecticut. Finding out what had gone wrong was the job of the utility engineers and the resident inspectors of the Nuclear Regulatory Commission. Actually doing the dirty work to fix the problem would fall to the mechanics employed by Trippler Power. The people in this room were the project supervisors who directed the union workers.

Alex waved and exchanged good-mornings with several of the supervisors. He headed for the far end of the office where several PCs and a couple of printers sat. While each project supervisor was responsible for perhaps hundreds of workers, Alex was responsible for hundreds of pounds of paper. So much paper, in fact, he'd often voiced the opinion that all nuke plants should be equipped to burn paper as auxiliary fuel. That way, the paper used to build them and fix them could be used to start the plants up.

His group generated the cost and performance reports as well as the incredibly detailed planning schedules, some of them timed down to the minute, of all the different tasks that had to be done while a nuclear plant was down for a maintenance outage.

Every day, every hour, that one of these mammoth plants wasn't producing electricity cost the utility stockholders dividends and ratepayers (the people who pay electric bills) a lot of money—money to buy replacement energy and money to pay the men and women working the outage. A general foreman pipe fitter working six twelve-hour shifts a week for a couple outages could easily pull down $120,000 in a year. The pace was murder, but it paid.

Alex didn't make that kind of money, but then neither did he have to spend ten hours a day out in the January cold. He also didn't have to worry about wearing a dosimeter to keep track of radiation exposure or be fitted for a respirator. That was one reason for the beard: it set him off from the jumpers, the people who made their money by jumping into the radioactive (or hot) areas to do necessary jobs, quickly using up their entire allowable exposure for a calendar quarter. Besides, the beard helped keep his face from freezing on the walk to and from the parking lot.

This part of the office was deserted. The rest of the office staff wouldn't be in for another hour or so. Alex came in early in order to prepare the morning reports so that the utility people could look them over while having their morning coffee.

Alex sat down at his desk and logged into his e-mail, looking for a message with a nightly report attached generated by the corporate mainframe that kept track of all of Trippler's projects. The e-mail was there, but there was no attachment. The nightly run at corporate had failed once again. That meant Alex's first job of the day, using that report to produce a summary for the project managers and the company reps, was going to be late once again.

Damn it all to hell, he muttered. *That puts me two hours behind, and the day hasn't even started yet.*

Alex wrote an e-mail to the corporate IT help desk, asking for a rerun, but those people wouldn't even be at their desks for another two hours.

While watching with only faint hope for a new message to pop up from some early bird at corporate, Alex started working on the summary report. About half the needed numbers were available, so it made sense to do as much as possible while waiting for the rest. The remainder of the day shift began to filter in as he sat there punching numbers into the spreadsheet. Some of the newcomers exchanged preoccupied greetings, along with smiles and groans about the cold. Another winter's day at the Point.

When the data input was finished, Alex headed for the coffeepot. The company had one gray-bearded, born-again laborer who cleaned the office and kept the coffee going. His name was Bear, and he made eighteen dollars an hour doing that. Trippler billed him to the utility at twice that rate.

One of the good things about working for the contractor: at least the coffee was free. Alex filled up his flat-bottomed captain's cup (bought after the one and only time he spilled his coffee into a keyboard) and went back to his desk.

Sitting there, staring at his computer screen, it was easy to forget about the cold and the wind outside, forget about the jobs that those numbers represented. Out there, men and women were acting as body servants to a single, huge machine, every part of which needed to run right all the time. Oh, a busted gauge didn't mean danger, but it could mean the NRC on your back, especially if it wasn't fixed right.

"Asleep again, Alex?" came a soft Southern voice from behind the musing computer man. He jumped enough that some of the coffee slopped over the rim and down the front of his flannel shirt.

"Damn it, Walker, do you always sneak up on people?" Alex asked while turning around. "It's got nothing to do with the noise in here. You walk like a cat, even in those clodhoppers!"

The sandy-haired man who had startled him gave a big grin. "Just trying to keep you on your toes, the job of any good supervisor. You got the morning report done yet? Or do I sense problems this morning?"

Walker James was the cost accounting supervisor and Alex's boss. Walker was a good six feet, two inches, broad faced, and freckled, but gaunt to the point of being almost skeletal. His job was to take the stuff Alex put out by the ton and show the utility where their money was going. He also had to explain the numbers to Trippler Power's management and, because of this, he was forever trapped in a crossfire. The utility wanted the work done on time and budget (or below) and Trippler's big bosses wanted to get every dime they could out of a job. After all, that was what paid their salaries.

"Yes, the nightly run at corporate screwed up again," Alex told him. "About half the input is done, and I'll finish it as soon as the rest of the data come through. Yes, the daily will be late, and you'll have to call the utility to let them know. Sorry."

"Okay, I hear you. Any ideas about why this shit keeps happening? This doesn't make us brownie points," Walker told him.

Alex shrugged, and a little more coffee sloshed. "No, that's above my pay grade. I have no idea what the system at corporate does to crunch those numbers."

Putting on a fine martyred expression, Alex finished, "I guess we'll just have to put up with a system that screws up just as bad as the old one but does it three times faster."

Walker laughed and headed off for his office, and Alex turned back to his screen. As he watched, an e-mail popped up that had the right attachment. *Hmm … Somebody got into corporate early this morning!* He quickly started pasting figures from the report into his spreadsheet.

The last part of this report always took the longest to input, because the new jobs were at the end, and there were six to add. As usual, the project supervisors hadn't given him all the information he needed, so he had to work the phone and the supervisors' bullpen to get it. Eventually, it got done.

After the morning report, there was the usual bitching about hardware problems and software bugs—people asking for help, people demanding help. Some of the timekeepers were pretty enough or sweet enough that it was a pleasure listening to them complain.

Alex was just finishing up a requisition when the phone rang. It was almost lunchtime, and the last thing he needed was another problem. "Trippler Power, Alex Strong," he said, trying to get the handset squeezed between shoulder and chin while trying to sign papers.

"Alex!" the voice on the phone said. "You sound like you're up to your ass in alligators again."

"Mr. Campbell, senior utility engineer, sir. How the hell are you?" The man on the line was Jacob "Jake" Campbell, Alex's oldest and best friend. He also happened to work for the customer. This call was the first bright spot of his morning.

"Less ragged than you are. I'm down here for the day. You got any plans for lunch, like I really need to ask?"

The contractor types got half an hour to eat. That meant either brown bagging it or a trip to the Roach Coach, the catering concession on-site.

"I was planning on eating in," he told Jake. "It's too damn cold to hike halfway across the plant for bad food. You want to come over here? I'll see if the conference room is free."

Jake chuckled over the line. "That's what I figured. Okay, I'll pick something up on the way over. See you in about ten minutes?"

"Great!" Alex told him. "It always gives my status around here a boost when a Yankee Power guy comes to pay me a visit! See you!" He hung up, scribbled a quick note on a requisition on his desk, and grabbed his lunch. As he headed for the conference room, he dropped the req into the in basket of the tool and materials man.

CHAPTER 2

JAKE CAMPBELL TURNED OFF THE COMPUTER sitting on his desk, grabbed his white hardhat, left his first floor cubicle, and headed out the door while shrugging into a coat. The wind made him catch his breath, but he jammed his hands into the pockets of the old navy watch coat and headed for the far side of the plant.

Four hours of weak, watery, winter sunshine hadn't done much to improve the day. Gray clouds covered most of the sky, and the wind coming off Long Island Sound was strong and raw. It carried a heavy odor of rotting sea life and salt.

Jake was a bigger, heavier, blond edition of his friend. With a white Yankee Power hardhat on his head, he towered over most of the people outside the Reactor Outage Building, or ROB. This two-story structure, with its corrugated steel skin, was home away from home for the utility engineers while a plant was down for maintenance. Inside, while still very crowded, it was much more comfortable than the contractors' quarters: solid walls, ceilings that didn't leak torrents, heaters that actually kept the place warm, and (to top it all off) indoor plumbing.

Since Unit III was almost a brand-new plant, not all the barriers left over from construction had been removed. Jake had to stand for a few seconds in yet another "doorframe." This one checked him and his clothing for radioactive contamination, and it was scheduled to be removed when the plant was fully operational.

Once through the checkpoint, it was a few more minutes to the Roach Coach. The flimsy shack was jammed with "green hats," the pipe fitters, welders, and members of a half-dozen other trades working the outage. Jake got his bag of greasy food and headed for the Trippler trailers, hurrying to get there before his food got cold.

Stepping into the Trippler offices, Jake found the controlled chaos he expected. For the hundredth time, he congratulated himself for getting a job with Yankee when he finished running nuclear missile subs for the United States Navy.

My cats live better than this, he thought as he squeezed down the aisle toward the one conference room.

Alex was already there, feet propped on a chair, as he used his smart phone to look at the latest tech headlines on CNET. Keeping on top of happenings in the computer world was as much fun for him as it was work. He looked up and smiled when his friend entered. Alex waved him to another chair. "Take a load off and get warmed up. Anything good at the Roach Coach?" he asked.

Pulling off his coat, Jake shrugged his shoulders. "Same old greasy shit," he said. "One of these days, we're going to have to find enough time to go off-site for lunch. What do you say?"

"Fine with me," Alex replied, "but let's wait until the weather warms up. Freezing my balls off on one round trip on days like this is already too much!"

Jake had to agree with the soundness of that. The parking lot for utility employees was a lot smaller than the contractor lot, but it would still be a cold hike. Eating became the main activity, but there was still a lot to talk about, like the newest and greatest computer gear. Jake had a computer science degree from CAL, but computers weren't his job like they were for Alex. He used them a lot, but when it came to programming them or fixing them he called somebody else, at least at the office. Jake was forever tinkering with his PC at home, always hooking up the latest gadget.

Jake started in about the latest tech addition to his household. "I love the new high-speed Internet connection they put in last week. The town is running fiber from the pole. When the weather is really cruddy, I can connect to the network in Hartford and still get some work done. I may not be able to get to everything, but I can check my e-mail and look at the plant status. That helps a lot. Of course, I could do that before, but this connection makes my old one look like a snail."

Alex was impressed by the technology but the rest of it ticked him off. The contractors didn't have that kind of access, and even if they did, the bottom line was pretty much that if they weren't on-site, they didn't get paid.

"You utility guys have it so easy," he told his friend. "You've got the access, you've got the resources, and you've got the flex time. Do ten-hour days, finish your forty hours for the week, and get a four-day weekend every other week. But what's this stuff about plant status? I knew you guys had a virtual private network set up with access to all your office apps, but this is news to me."

"Yeah, it's something new," Jake mumbled around a brownie. "It's a graphical front end that somebody in the head shed cooked up. Depending on your access rights, you can look at a lot of stuff. You get a map of the plant then click on a building. That gives you a plan of the building. Then you can click on rooms, floors, whatever, and get details. Click on a turbine building, and you can see both the high- and low-pressure systems. Then you can click on either one and see what the RPMs are, what the inlet and outlet temps are, all that good stuff."

"Holy crap," Alex responded. "How long did it take them to work all that out? How the hell do they get all the data?"

"Data are the easy part," said Jake. "All the instrumentation was really already in place. After all, you're just looking at the same stuff the guys in the control room see, and it all gets to the control room on a LAN. It's just that you can't push any buttons over the VPN and scram the plant!"

"Bloody well better not," was Alex's response. "That would be taking it too far." Changing the subject, he asked, "It's Thursday, so does your weekend start tomorrow? Got any plans?"

"Not really," replied Jake. "It's still too damn snowy and cold to be doing outside work. I've got a new pellet stove I want to put in, and Susan wants to drive out to Stockbridge to see her brother. Why don't you come out and join us?"

"Can't do it," came the exasperated growl. "They put me on six twelves starting this week. I can certainly use the money, but the schedule sucks.

I guess it's still better than the thirteen days on, one off that the trades get during an outage peak, but it still sucks. When was the last time you had to work a schedule like that?"

"It was when the Haddam Neck plant was down last year. The next time will be when Unit I here goes down, sometime next fall. You're right. Twelve-hour shifts are not fun, but at least you have a lot shorter drive than I do. I'm commuting all the way from Middletown. You're just down the road in Waterford."

Alex made a sour face then said, "True, but there's not much to do in that dinky little apartment. I'm glad the divorce is over and done with, but the house was a lot more comfortable. I guess it will have to do for now."

"Well, when you can get free, let me know. I know Susan would like to see you, and there's always a place for you to crash."

Jake stood, crumpled up his trash, and threw it in the nearest trashcan. He gave a big stretch, almost reaching both walls of the little conference room, and then reached for his coat. "Time for me to move it. I got in early so five hours more and I'm outta here."

"Six more for me," said his friend, who walked him to the door, wished him a good weekend, and returned to his desk.

Alex's routine called for updating numbers on the largest projects based on information from the project supervisors about the morning's work. Final hours worked would come from the nightly run done at corporate after the day's time sheets were entered. That process took him another half hour, but then some new jobs got dropped on his desk to be set up.

One of these drew his attention. *Whew, this is a big one and it's not a maintenance job. It's new construction! Since when do we do that?*

He walked over to Walker's office and knocked on the doorframe. Walker looked up from the pile of drawings on his desk and motioned him in.

"What's up?" he asked.

"It's this new job that just came in. I've never seen us do new construction here. What is this thing? How should I cost it out?"

Walker gave a brief smile. "It's a new building they're calling the 're-rack' building. It's going to be used for stacking fuel rod bundles for storage or shipment out. It's not in the original plant design for any of the reactors, so it doesn't come under any of the construction contracts. It went up for bid and we got it. It's just a sheet-metal structure over a steel frame with a concrete floor. There's an overhead crane that runs on a rail system separate from the trusses. It should go together easy. But there's one thing about it that's going to be a pain in the ass."

"What's that?" Alex asked him.

"The project manager for the utility is Frank Spencer. I *know* how happy that's going to make everybody involved with this, including you!"

When he heard that dreaded name, Alex let out a groan of pain. "Not him! That man is the angriest person I've ever met. He walks around all day just below boiling point, barely holding back from popping off like Unit III did this morning. He's the last person from Yankee that anybody here wants to work with, period. Can't we dump him?"

"Not a snowball's chance," his boss replied. "We're stuck with him. At least you just generate the reports. Some of us have to really work with the man!"

"If he doesn't like the numbers he sees," Alex retorted, "he'll be pounding on my desk asking why they aren't as predicted and he won't listen when I say I don't do estimates or scheduling, I just report what the project supes give me. Do me a favor and remind him that he has no right to ride my ass. That's your privilege, and he has to go through channels!"

"I will, I promise." Then he changed the subject. "Are the midday data in?"

"I'm going to hold you to that. Yes, they're in. After I get the new jobs entered from the planners, I should be about done for the day, but I'm not supposed to leave until six."

"Finish that crap up, come back, and let's go over the new stuff. By then, it should be time to call it a day."

"You got it, boss. Back to my keyboard." Alex turned and headed to the noise of the bullpen.

Alex finished with new projects, had another cup of coffee, and then had his meeting with Walker. After that, it was time to bundle up and reverse the morning process of entering the plant: brass out, hike to the MAP, drop off his badge, and find his truck in the lot. One more day as a single cell working to feed the huge organism that was Osprey Point.

As his friend had mentioned at lunch, Alex didn't live far from the plant. His dinky little apartment was just over three miles from the turnoff. The one-bedroom place was at the top of a house of an older couple. It was comfortable, convenient, and came furnished right down to pots, pans, and plates. Evidently, it rented frequently to men like Alex who were getting divorced or just done with the chore.

Alex pulled his truck around the back of the house, got out, and walked around the front to get his mail. Not surprisingly, there really wasn't anything important. He was looking for jobs outside of New England but no bites yet, and nothing had come in on his phone e-mail during the day.

He walked, more like trudged, up the long flight of stairs to his door. Fumbling with the keys in his heavily gloved hands, he finally got the door open and entered the little dining area. Off to the right were the kitchen and a door that led to the bedroom. To the left was the bathroom, and straight ahead was the living room, which strangely had a large, open archway into the bedroom that ran front to back of the apartment. He dropped his hat, coat, and gloves onto a chair at the dinette table then headed to the kitchen to make a cup of decaf.

Coffee in hand, he settled deeply into the one armchair in the living room and turned on the TV. Right now, cable was pretty much his only luxury and he punched the number for the channel running a *Firefly* marathon. *A little sci-fi, some leftovers, and then bed. Two more days until a day off …*

CHAPTER 3

SATURDAY FINALLY ARRIVED, AND AT 6:00 PM Alex's seventy-two-hour week ended. As he shut down his computer and got ready to leave, the glare of the overhead fluorescent tubes showed the tired look on his face and the circles under his brown eyes. He sat with his head in his hands for a few moments, trying to decide whether to just head home or stop and get dinner on the way. Most of the project staffers didn't live in the area, some were married and just wanted to get home. So whatever he did, he was going to do it on his own.

As he sat there, a thought suddenly came to him. *My divorce has been final for a month, and I haven't celebrated that at all! I'm going to go out and have a couple of drinks, a good dinner, and maybe even talk to a pretty woman!*

Alex made his way through the torturous maze he had to navigate to leave the plant. Once he was in his truck and on the access road, he turned left on Rope Ferry Road, heading for Niantic and East Lyme instead of turning right, back toward the center of Waterford and his apartment. Just before reaching the bridge, he turned right and was very quickly in the parking lot of a trendy-looking place called the Sunset Ribs Co. It served up the best short ribs in the state, and they were one of his all-time favorite things to eat.

He hurried in from the cold, stopping to shove his gloves, scarf, and hat into the deep front pockets of his winter coat. Peeling it off, he hung it on one of the hooks by the door.

The tables were almost all empty. During the summer, the Sunset catered to the tourist trade and yachting types. Business really slowed down in the off-season, and the place even closed for part of the winter.

Alex stood at the hostess's desk and considered. *I can sit at a table by myself, but food's not the only reason I came here. It'll be nice to be around somebody besides engineers and construction workers for a while.*

As the hostess came up to him, the two of them exchanged smiles but Alex motioned that he was heading for the bar. She nodded in reply and he turned toward the large mahogany bar, actually almost full, and took a seat.

The bartender was an old acquaintance, an expat Aussie who had been in the states for twenty years or so. The blond hostess with the big boobs was his wife.

"Hey there, Pete. How's business?" Alex asked while wiggling himself on to the high bar stool.

"Alex!" the barkeep smiled back. "Been a long time, mate. Where the hell have you been? Where's the missus?"

"It's been longer than I thought if you don't know we split up. The divorce was final a month ago. I've been so drowned with work I just haven't had a chance to come in. Finally got a Saturday night off and decided to celebrate with a couple of bourbon-and-sevens and some ribs. Is the smoker going?"

"Hey, man, sorry to hear about that, but shit like that happens. Yeah, the barbie's been going all day and I've got ribs just begging to be eaten up. You like the beef ribs, right?"

Alex gave a shrug and then agreed about the split and the ribs. "But before I start chowing down on your finest, let me have that drink first, would you please?"

"Coming right up," the barkeep called over his shoulder as he reached for a bottle of Basil Hayden's on the shelf behind him.

"Hey, don't be so fast with the expensive hooch. Jim Beam'll do just fine."

"No sweat, mate. First one's on the house on account of the divorce. You should have come in sooner. Dollars to doughnuts you've been seeing a shrink, right? Cheaper to come here!"

"That may be true," Alex answered with a chuckle in his voice, something very rare for him over the last few months. "But getting soused on a regular basis isn't going help me get up at oh-five-double-dark six days a week."

"Poor sod," came the sarcastic reply as the drink, a double, ended up on the bar in front of Alex. "Try running a place like this someday. You'll find out what work really is."

Alex laughed at the barkeep and put on his worst Aussie accent. "Too right, cobber. Think I'm wonky enough for that?" Dropping the act, he continued. "Thanks very much for the expensive booze and let me have a plate of the short ribs with corn bread and coleslaw. And don't you go walkabout getting them here!"

"After that, you'll be lucky to ever get another drop!" came Pete's retort. "Bonzer, we'll have them for you in no time. Or do you want some time with that stuff you Americans call whiskey first?"

"Give me a minute. I just got out of the plant and need to decompress a bit. No rush."

"Drink that down, and we'll get you your tucker straight away," Pete told him before turning to his other customers.

Alex sipped the whiskey slowly, amazed at the smoothness and depth of the liquid on his tongue. *This stuff comes from the same people that make Jim Beam but you'd never guess it. I could get hooked on this …*

Using the mirror in front of him, Alex took the time to look over the other patrons of the bar. They were a mixed lot. He was pretty sure some of them were people from the Point he did not know. Some of them appeared to be workers from the boatyards in the area. A few were locals like him, maybe yachting types looking over their boats, dreaming of warmer weather and long sails.

As Alex looked back at his own reflection, he noticed a movement behind him. The newcomer had to come closer before he could see she was a pretty, light-skinned African American woman. *Not pretty; she's drop-dead gorgeous.* Her features, along with what he judged to be a luscious *café au lait* shade of skin, made him think her parentage was mixed. *White mother or father?* he wondered. *Whichever it is, she's the most beautiful thing I've seen in a long time. Twenty-something? Must be, or she wouldn't be in the bar,* he mused some more.

The woman stepped around to the waitress station and waved Pete down. "Hi, Pete," she called. "Got my take-out order ready?"

Pete loved a pretty sheila and gave her a big smile. "Too right, luv," he told her. "Got it right here." He reached out for a big paper bag sitting on the counter behind the bar. After a quick glance at the slip, he told the young woman the price. She paid him and told him to keep the change.

As she turned to go, her deep, brown eyes met Alex's for a moment and they exchanged quick smiles. Then she was on her way out the door. Looking into the mirror, Alex could watch her leave. And while it was hard to tell with the winter coat she was wearing, he got the impression the view from the back was as good as the one from the front.

Pete saw him watching her in the mirror. "Don't even think on it, mate. Too soon for you, and she's probably more than you could handle. Dances over at Rosie's, she does. Stops in here once in a while to pick up dinner for her and her mates. Must burn it all off onstage though."

"Rosie's? Really? Strippers are getting younger every day. Or more likely we're getting older."

"Too right. Another reason you're not likely to bail her up. Hey, here comes Angie with your tucker."

Glancing up in the mirror again, Alex saw a brunette waitress heading toward the bar with a big platter. He leaned back to give her room to set it down, smiled his thanks at her, and gave a gluttonous gaze at the best meal he'd even seen in months. "Enjoy," Pete told him. "Need another drink?"

"Just water with this, thanks. I'll have another later. Looks great, Pete."

"You just let me know if it isn't," Pete replied. "We'll make it right."

Alex set to his meal, but as he took his first bite of rib, his thoughts were on the girl, not the food. *I wonder what her name is.*

As expected, the ribs were excellent, and it was nice to be around some different people, especially when the alternative was sitting alone in his little apartment. He took his time, savoring every bite, and finally had the ribs down to very bare bones.

Pete cleared away his platter and said, "Don't have to ask you if you liked that, do I? Want another drink before you toddle off?"

"Yeah, let me have a single of that good stuff. I'll sit here and nurse it and let dinner settle before I head home. As usual, Pete, it was great. Just what I needed."

As Alex sipped the bourbon, his mind drifted back to the girl who had made such an impression earlier. "Hey, Pete, be a good mate and tell me the name of that girl from Rosie's."

"Can't do it, Alex," he replied. "She's too much for you to handle. If you want to know, you're going to have to go find out on your own."

"Some pal you are!" said Alex. "Well, it's time for this old boy to head on home. See you soon, Pete."

With that, Alex retrieved his coat, hit the remote starter on the truck to start getting it warmed up against the January chill, and headed for the door.

I'll have make a field trip to Rosie's just as soon as things settle down, he thought as he stepped out into the cold.

CHAPTER 4

ALEX LOOKED WISTFULLY BACK AT THAT evening over the next few weeks. The outage, along with the normal maintenance work and special projects, kept everybody jumping, sometimes literally, for that whole time. Eventually, the outage wound down and hours got cut back.

But there was one job that just refused to go right.

It was a Friday morning in February, still cold and raw with temperatures below freezing, and Alex was working on a weekly roll-up report for a management meeting scheduled right after lunch. He worked his way through the numbers from corporate, adding in the estimates from the project managers, when he suddenly came to some numbers that were completely out of left field.

This is the re-rack building. That was at 80 percent and now it's back down to 50 percent! The whole estimate is twice what it was and the completion date from the PM has been pushed way the hell out! What is going on here?

Alex left his desk and headed for Walker's office. The door was open and he could see Walker was head down over some plans spread across his desk. Alex's knock made Walker look up, but it was obvious from his stare that he hadn't shifted gears yet.

"You busy?" Alex asked. "I can come back later, but this has to do with the meeting in a couple hours."

It was intriguing, watching Walker move the drawings out of his mind and turn his attention to Alex. "What's up?" he asked.

"Just what the hell is going on with the re-rack building? It dropped from 80 percent to 50 percent complete, the scope has expanded, and the drop-dead date has been pushed out two months! What happened?" he demanded.

"You haven't heard?" Walker responded, pretty needlessly. "The client got the specs wrong! They gave a specific height, we built it that way, and now it turns out it's too damn short!" After a derisive snort, Walker continued, "They say they gotta have the building, so what they want now is for us to jack it up, pour a six-foot-tall cast concrete wall for the beams and sheet metal to sit on, and plop it down on top of that!"

Instantly, Alex's mind could see ripple effect this caused and he broke out laughing. Finally catching his breath, he said to Walker, "It's too damn cold out there to pour concrete, so we have to tent and preheat to pour all that wall! Especially because it has to meet NRC spec! They are bloody lucky we haven't poured the floor, or we'd have to jack-hammer the wall thickness away too!" Normal procedure in cold weather was to get the building tight, heated, and then pour the slab. "Who's going to get the blame for this one? It'd better not be us, if we followed the drawings."

Walker wasn't as amused as Alex, but he did smile when he heard the final comment. "No, it's not us. It's your favorite utility PM: Frank Spencer."

That news brought another round of laughter from Alex. "Oh my God, that's great. Has *he* gotten the news yet? I want to see how red he gets when he finds out!"

"Sorry, he already knows. However, I'm sure he'll get raked over the coals during the project update meeting if you want to come and sit in a corner to watch the fireworks. You can pretend to pass me reports or something. But I don't know if the show is worth your time and Big Mike will probably end up asking me why you don't have anything better to do." Big Mike was Mike Stuart, Trippler's top manger at Osprey Point.

"I'll skip it, thanks," Alex replied. "I've got enough to keep me going right up to lunch and maybe then some. I'll have the roll-up report for you in thirty minutes."

Walker gave him a Southern-boy shit-eating grin and told him he knew that meant twenty. "Now get out so I can get ready myself!" Walker put his head down again, looking at the drawings on his desk, as Alex turned to leave, but not before noticing that the drawings on the desk were for the very project that was causing all the trouble.

It turned out that Alex didn't need to sit in on the meeting to hear the fireworks. The mobile office walls were thin and stopped sound about as well as tissue paper. The noise started as a low rumble and built to what sounded like a three-way shouting match. The voices belonged to Big Mike, Frank Spencer, and Frank's boss, some corporate big shot from the utility's HQ in Hartford. About the time the noise increased to the catfight level, it suddenly stopped and people started coming out of the conference room like it was a movie theater on fire. Spencer was the second one out. *He's not even his usual shade of red,* thought Alex. *He's actually blotchy! I'm amazed he hasn't had a stroke!*

After the Yankee Power people left the building and Big Mike returned to his corner office, Alex made his way over to talk to Walker. His boss looked up when Alex knocked on the doorframe, motioned him to come in, and then gave a push of his hand for Alex to shut the door.

"I've never heard a commotion like that in the eleven months I've been here," Alex commiserated.

"Twelve years I've been in this business and I haven't either," Walker confided. "They really wanted to dump all the problems on us, but there was no way Big Mike was going to put up with that crap. The specs and the drawings are as plain as day. They fucked it up, especially Spencer because he was the final approver. Sure, he just pencil-whipped it, figuring the designers had gotten it all down pat, but it's his initials in the block. Somebody did the arithmetic wrong and he didn't catch it. That's just too damn bad for Yankee Power and Frank Spencer in particular."

"Are we going to finish the work, or are they going to move it in-house and try to save a few bucks while screwing us at the same time?" Alex asked his boss.

"It's still in our court. But I'm going to talk to all the project supervisors and tell them to watch every goddamn minute that goes into that job. You too. If you see anything that looks out of whack, let me know ASAP. We can't give the customer the smallest excuse to hang us on this. They will if they can and break our contract for cause."

"You got it, boss. I will watch every penny that goes through and I'll set up a trend analysis to keep watch on how fast the money is being spent."

"Good," Walker agreed. "Now if you will get the hell outta here, I want to put that fiasco behind me. And now that we're down to five tens and it's Friday, I want to leave on time."

"I'm with you on that one. If I don't see you before quitting time, have a good weekend."

Alex returned to his desk and found a trouble ticket waiting from Patricia Sobel, one of the lead field accountants. Grabbing his "go bag" of tools and spares, he headed for her desk in the next trailer over where the site accountants lived. While Patricia was one of his favorite people on the site, Alex wanted to help her quickly so he could go on his way.

Patricia saw Alex heading down the center aisle, smiled at him, and waved. She was a short, plump brunette who was always in a good mood no matter what crap was flowing downhill.

Alex reached the desk, they exchanged hellos, and then Patricia told him that her PC wouldn't start up when she came back from a visit to the brass shack.

"Mind letting me drive?" Alex asked her. She got up from her chair and let him squeeze by. He sat down, pushed the power button on the PC, and got nothing. Then he noticed that the monitor was dead too. *Okay, I know where this is going.* Reaching over to her desk lamp, he flicked the switch on that too: nothing happened.

"Patty, you've got no power to your whole desk. Is the power strip even plugged into the wall?" Alex asked her.

Patricia wiggled behind her desk to where she could see the cords. "Yes, it's plugged in and it's turned on, but there's no light on it."

Alex grunted a response, reached down, and grabbed a spare strip from his bag. The power to the Trippler trailers was notoriously dirty, something of an irony seeing as how they were located at a power plant. Spikes routinely took out surge suppressors in this place. He handed the new strip to her, since she was already back there with the wires, and asked her to swap it out and let him know if it didn't do the trick. They wished each other a good weekend and Alex headed back to the bullpen to close the ticket and get ready to head home. *I wish they were all that simple,* he thought as he walked down the aisle.

Glancing at the clock on his computer desktop, Alex decided by the time he got to the brass shack it would be five and he could brass out. He checked his mail one last time, cleared a few papers from his desk, and then started to turn off his PC. With his finger poised to click on the shutdown icon an idea suddenly popped into his mind. *Damn, this is my first full weekend off in a couple of months. Maybe tonight is a good night to raise a little hell. But what to do?*

He brought up Google and did a quick search on Rosie's in East Lyme. Using company computers to look up strip clubs was against policy, but since he was the person who set up the firewall and filters for the Osprey Point site, he had very carefully exempted his personal MAC address from all restrictions. It actually was necessary so he could download software, patches, and visit support sites forbidden to regular users. It also came in handy for other reasons.

Clicking on the Google link popped up Rosie's home page. There was a link for hours, and it showed they opened at three on Friday afternoons. Decision made, he shut down, got into his coat and hat, and headed out into the rapidly darkening late February day.

CHAPTER 5

As he had a few weeks ago, Alex made the left toward East Lyme instead of the right toward his apartment. Before reaching the bridge, he turned right, went past Sunset Ribs, his main watering hole, and continued on a couple of short blocks to Rosie's.

There were only a few cars in the lot at this early hour, but the neon sign was already lit. The name was spelled out in yellow with a red flower at the end. *It's supposed to be a rose*, Alex thought, *but it looks more like a carnation.*

After getting out of the truck, Alex tossed his hat, gloves, and Leatherman onto the passenger seat. Reaching into his left pants pocket, he did a quick count of his cash. *It's not much, but it should get me started ...*

The first people he saw as he walked into the club were a bouncer and a coat-check girl who also collected the cover charge and checked IDs. Pulling out his wallet, he showed his license, kept his coat, and asked what the cover was. The girl behind the counter smiled, thanked him, and told him there was no cover before six. *That's a good start.*

Stepping through the next set of doors, Alex took off his coat and paused a minute to let his eyes adjust. It wasn't very bright outside, but it was really dim in here. His first sweep was to count heads, and he found very few people in the club. The second one was more to get the lay of the land. He'd only been in here once, years ago for a bachelor party, and the place had changed a lot. The bar was to his left. The stage (two poles) was in front of him and a little left of the entrance, surrounded by a very narrow counter that had chairs pushed up against it. Outside of that ring

25

were some low tables and chairs, while back toward the bar were high tables with tall chairs.

Something unfamiliar caught his eye. Behind the tables surrounding the stage, right up against the mirrored walls on either side, were bench seats, up high, almost like a stadium. He cataloged that for further thought and continued his look around.

Off to the right was another room, gauzy curtains blocking the view. This was obviously the VIP room. To the left of that was a hallway that had a RESTROOMS sign with an arrow, and as his gaze swept by, he noticed a blond wearing a skimpy costume in red and silver with six-inch silver platforms come out of an unmarked door. *Probably the dancers' dressing room.*

Other than that one dancer, the place was basically empty. *What the hell? It's still early.*

Over at the bar was one bartender (female, brunette, tallish, and wearing a black bustier), and a blond who was probably a waitress. Without her heels, Alex guessed the waitress at about five feet nothing. She was wearing a little baby-doll outfit, the color uncertain in the poor light. She looked like the girl next-door at a slumber party. The one guy at the bar didn't look like a customer, another big and burly sort. The way he was talking to the girls, Alex guessed he was the manager.

Alex picked a low table toward the bar end, near the stage but not right up against it. He preferred this kind of spot, mostly because it gave him a better view of the surroundings.

Suddenly, the speakers started blaring out a number by Snake River Conspiracy, not one of Alex's favorite bands, and the DJ, in a little booth near the bar, started saying something just as loud and completely unintelligible. The dim lighting started getting pierced by flashing colored spots, and little red laser dots started spinning around the room.

The blond dancer Alex had noticed when he came in walked by, giving him a brief look as she passed. At the far end of the room, she disappeared behind a curtain, emerging a few seconds later on the stage. Evidently, SRC was *her* thing, because she began moving to the rhythm.

The waitress appeared at that moment, giving Alex a big smile and laying a napkin down on the little table. Leaning close and shouting in his ear, she asked what he wanted to drink. Deciding to start off easy, Alex gave her a smile back and shouted back, "Diet Coke!" She nodded and headed off to the bar.

The dancer, meanwhile, had moved up to his end of the stage and was giving him a private show, easy to do since he was the only customer in the place. He guessed she'd be about five foot two without the platforms, very slender, almost too thin.

A break in the music and the return of the waitress came at the same time. Placing the glass on the table, she said, "That's four dollars, honey." He reached into his pocket, peeled off a twenty, and handed it to her. She made change, all in singles of course, and handed it to him. Giving her a couple back, he asked her name.

"Alanna," she told him. "What's yours, honey? First time here?"

"Alex," he told her, "and it's my first time in a long time. The place has changed some."

He really couldn't hear her answer as the music started up again. Alanna leaned down to his ear and shouted, "It's the way it was when I started here a couple months ago! Let me know if you need anything else, honey!" She turned and headed back to the bar, her cute little backside swaying below the baby-doll top.

The music started up again and the front doors opened up at the same time. A gaggle of young women came in but, with the stage lights in his eyes, Alex couldn't make out any details. All of them headed for the hallway and disappeared into what Alex had tagged in his mind as door #3.

He turned his attention back to the stage just as the blond finished untying her sparkling red bra and tossing it onto the stage. *Not bad. A little on the skinny side for me, but not bad at all, especially considering the drought I've been in for the last few months!*

Alex got up and walked to the stage. He smiled at the blond dancer but didn't get much in return. He bent down to lay three dollar bills on the edge of the runway. When he looked up, he could see the dancer mouthing a thank-you at him, and he went back to his seat to watch the show and sip his soda.

This time, in the break between songs, he was pretty sure he heard the

DJ give the dancer's name as Sparkle. *That fits. I wonder if all her costumes glitter like that. Must be a trademark.*

Last song of the set, and he got a very good look as the last of Sparkle's costume went sliding down to the stage. As the only customer in the club, Alex got an eyeful.

As Sparkle gathered up her clothes (what there were of them) and headed for the curtain, the DJ went into a commercial about welcome to Rosie's, most beautiful dancers anywhere and more general BS. It was evidently shift change and more girls would be onstage soon.

Sparkle appeared from behind the ground-level curtain and headed straight for Alex's table. As she approached, he got up and held out his hand to meet hers.

"Thank you, sweetie," she said. Then in a rush came, "Can I join you? What's your name? Mine's Sparkle."

"Sure," replied Alex, and he gestured to the other chair. Catching Alanna's eye, he waved her over. Unfortunately, she got there just as the music started up again and it was another shouting match to find out that Sparkle wanted a glass of white wine.

The drink showed up quickly and the two of them made shouted chitchat. After a few minutes, Alex decided to ask her about the elevated seats against the walls on each side of the stage.

"That's where we do lap dances, honey. And where the massage girls give back rubs. Would you like a dance? It's twenty dollars for each song."

Alex quickly decided that the gallery was way too public for him but told Sparkle that he just wanted to sit and look the place over, see what the ladies were like, and chill a while.

Sparkle finished her drink then told him she had to change for her next number. She thanked him and headed off for the dressing room, stopping on the way to talk to people at the bar.

Alex sat through a couple of more sets as new dancers came out and the crowd started to build. Some of the guys were obviously regulars. The way the dancers greeted them, played up to them onstage, and went directly over to their tables after their sets made that obvious.

One dancer, definitely older than the others, caught Alex's eye. It wasn't so much her looks, though she was better built than anyone he'd seen so far. No, it was her shoes! Alex couldn't believe it when she walked by to get to the stage. Her platforms were lighting up with every step; LEDs flashing blue, green, yellow and red, just like the shoes you see little kids begging their mothers for at the mall. It was hilarious and certainly got his attention. When she started dancing, they actually seemed to flash in time with the music. It was mesmerizing.

Just as this dancer (Tanya, according to the DJ) was finishing up her last number, the DJ Otter remix of "Boys of Summer," a flash of white over in the hallway caught Alex's eye. He glanced over and then did a classic double take. It was the woman from the restaurant!

She was wearing a white, silky halter dress with a large glittering buckle on the attached white belt. It instantly reminded Alex of the dress Marilyn Monroe wore in *Some Like It Hot,* the scene where she lets the air from the subway shaft blow up her skirt. The effect of the white material against her brown skin was stunning. The image of a dark-skinned Marilyn was reinforced by the fact that the dancer's hair was styled in very much the same fashion Marilyn wore in the movie. Her build was very similar as well, perhaps a little bustier. *God, she's pretty. This one I've got to get to know a little better.*

The dancer stood at the entrance to the main floor while checking out the room. As her gaze swept past, their eyes locked for a moment. Then hers moved on to examine the rest of the crowd. It wasn't a cursory sweep. More like the sort of survey he'd done when he arrived, searching for detail, memorizing the space. *Interesting.*

After a few more seconds she moved over to one of the tall tables closer to the bar and joined a tall brunette with very long legs wearing hot pink and a very big smile. After exchanging a quick hug, she sat down and gave Alanna a drink order.

By this point, Alex had fended off a couple of more dance offers and switched over to Sam Adams instead of Diet Coke. This didn't seem like the kind of place to go heavy on the hard stuff, so he was content to nurse the beer and watch the show.

Some of the men present didn't share his dislike for the bleacher seats (as he'd come to think of them) and were getting lap dances from the girls.

Alex was amazed to see the dancers were really stripping down and grinding away. He didn't recall that kind of action the first time he was here.

A set ended just as he finished his second beer. The DJ made another incomprehensible announcement and the girl in the white dress got up and headed for the stage. As she passed his table, she stopped and smiled at him. He stood up and discovered that, in her platforms, she was actually a bit taller.

"I know you from somewhere," she said, "but not here."

Alex was amazed she could remember a passing encounter like that. "I saw you for all of two minutes at the Sunset a few weeks ago. Pete told me you worked here, but this is the first chance I've had to stop by."

"You were sitting at the bar," she replied. "I remember now." And just then "Heard It through the Grapevine" started up. "I've got to get onstage!" she shouted. "Thanks for coming!"

And she was gone.

Alex sat down as the young woman disappeared behind the curtain and reappeared onstage. She took a few moments to wipe down the poles and then went into her first dance. Alex watched her closely, seeing how the dress she wore swished as she moved, flying up during her pirouettes just like Marilyn's in the subway blasts. Her legs were just right for her—not too long. The shoes obviously added a lot of height but didn't keep her from moving well.

When the first number was over, Alex stood up, peeled a five-dollar bill from his rapidly diminishing roll, and laid it on the stage rail. She saw him and came over to where he stood then kneeled down so that her face was just about level with his.

"Thank you, sweetie. I'm Charlie. What's your name?" she asked him, delivering a dazzling smile that showed perfect white teeth.

"Alex," he replied. "Can I buy you a drink after your set?"

"I'd love that. I'll come sit with you when I'm done. Thanks again."

Alex went back to his chair as she went into her second number, undoing the halter around her neck and playing peek-a-boo with the top while "Play That Funky Music" blared from the speakers. At the end of the song, she let the dress slip down to the floor, leaving her in a white and silver G-string. Once the third song started, that didn't last long.

CHAPTER 6

CHARLIE FINISHED UP HER LAST NUMBER, slipped back into her costume, and left the stage. The next dancer hadn't even started before she was at Alex's table. Once again, he stood up to greet her and held the chair for her as she sat down.

"An old-fashioned gentleman," she said.

"You're welcome. Can I get you something?" Alex caught Alanna's eye and waved her over. Charlie ordered a Grey Goose dirty martini in a rocks glass and Alex opted for another beer.

While waiting for the drinks to arrive, Charlie took the lead on the conversation. "So you haven't been here before?" she asked.

"Not for a long time. A friend of mine had a bachelor party here years ago. The place looks a lot different. The party was back in the VIP room; no idea if that's changed." He waved a hand toward the bleachers and continued. "Those seats up against the walls weren't there, for example. Can't say I care for them very much," he told her.

"I heard the last remodeling job was done about a year ago," Charlie informed him. "I can guess why you don't like the lap dance seats. Too open, right?"

"You got it. I'm really a bit of a prude," Alex admitted.

"Well, for one hundred dollars, you can get three dances back in the VIP room. It's a lot more private." She stated it as a matter of fact, not a sell job.

"I'll keep that in mind," Alex told her. "So are you from around here?"

"I grew up in Rhode Island," Charlie told him. "I'm a senior at Conn College."

"Studying what?" he asked.

"You won't believe me if I tell you," was Charlie's response, along with a sly grin.

"Try me," Alex encouraged.

"Well, I'm studying criminal justice with a concentration in forensic science," she admitted with a watchful look, waiting to catch his reaction.

"So your goal is to be a real-life Catherine Willows?" he asked, referring to the character from *CSI* who worked as a stripper before joining the Las Vegas crime lab.

"You bet!" Charlie came back. "I'm just getting my cop training in school instead of from one of my customers."

"That explains something I noticed when you walked in from the dressing room," Alex told her. "I saw you stop and really look the place over. I bet you could have told me the location of every person in the club. That also explains how you remembered me from Pete's place. Impressive."

"They try and teach us to be good observers," she told him. "But you said you remembered me too. How did that happen?"

"Easy. First, there weren't many people in the restaurant, and even bundled up in your winter coat, you were the prettiest woman in the place." The compliment earned him a smile. "Second, even though I'm a computer geek now, my degree is in psychology. The chairman of the department was really big on learning theory and all our professors taught us techniques for observation and memory. It's come in handy over the years."

"That makes sense," she said. Then a change of subject. "Where do you work?"

"Over at Osprey Point. I work for the maintenance contractor, Trippler Power. I do cost tracking and analysis, plus I'm the computer support guy for our people on-site."

"How did you go from psychology to computers? That's a big jump."

Alex shrugged his shoulders and told her, "No money for grad school and I had to make a living. I went nights to the tech school up in Norwich, and that got me my first computer job. I had a wife and two stepkids to support, so I did what I had to do. Even so, it didn't work out and my divorce was final a couple months ago." Alex had no idea why he was blurting all this stuff out, but it just poured from his mouth. Maybe it was those beautiful brown eyes that never left his.

"Sorry to hear that," Charlie told him. "No kids of your own?" she queried.

"No, thank God. That made everything a lot easier. When I moved out, I didn't even change my ZIP Code. I have a little apartment just a couple miles from here, top floor of an older couple's house. It's a nice place, but I hardly spent any time there at first. We've been in outage mode until just recently, and that means sixty hours a week, or even more."

"That's worse than here!" she exclaimed. "No wonder you didn't have time to drop by."

Alex gave Charlie an appreciative glance then told her, "I'm glad I finally made it. You are prettier than I remembered, and I really like your costume." Then he told her about the resemblance to Marilyn Monroe that had occurred to him when he saw her walk in.

Charlie gave him another of her thousand-lumen smiles, along with a cute tuck of her chin and a few bats of her eyes. "Thank you, sir. Believe it or not, I was an ugly duckling until my last year of high school. Ninety-five pounds soaking wet, braces, and no boobs. That all started to change about halfway through senior year." Then she asked, "Would you like to go outside with me? I'm up again soon and I'd like to have a cigarette before I do."

"Lead the way," Alex replied.

He grabbed his coat while Charley ducked into the DJ booth and grabbed a wrap. He followed her toward the back of the stage where he noticed another door. It led outside to a rudimentary patio, about twelve by eighteen, surrounded by panel fencing. There were a couple of tall patio tables, some butt receptacles, and not much else. A few other dancers were out there smoking, accompanied by two men: one biker type, one senior citizen. Charlie pulled a pack of smokes and a lighter out of her purse and then got a look on her face somewhere between astonishment and confusion as Alex took the lighter from her hand and lit her cigarette for her.

She took a big long drag then, while giving him a penetrating look, breathed it out. In a wondering tone, she told him, "I've been working here for almost two years, and that's the first time any guy has done that for me. What planet are you from?"

Alex gave her a rueful sort of grin and confessed, "I was born in Virginia. I was brought up to be a gentleman. And if you want my real opinion, most men are jerks and have absolutely no idea of how to be nice to a lady. Their brains are stuck in the Stone Age and they think all they need to do is carry a club, swear a lot, and women will fall all over them."

Charlie laughed and said, "I never quite thought about it that way before. Even if you're not 100 percent right, it's still a nice change. What brought you to Connecticut? It's a long way from Virginia."

Alex shook his head. "I didn't come here from Virginia," he told her. "I'm an army brat. I was born there, but my family moved around a lot. I mostly grew up out in the desert in California. I came out here because I was having a tough time finding work out west and my best friend, a guy I've known since junior high, bought me a plane ticket to Connecticut and let me live with him while I looked for a job." He knew he was running at the mouth, but there was something about her attentive gaze that encouraged him to blab away.

"He was in the navy at the time, teaching at the Naval Submarine School in Groton, and had just gotten divorced himself. A few months after I moved here, I met my ex-to-be, got married, and went through several gigs before settling into computers. That seems to be working out for me."

Charlie finished up her cigarette with one last drag, tossed the butt, and pulled her wrap tighter. *"Brr!* It's cold out here! We better go in before I freeze, and it's almost time for my next set."

They headed back in and did a little dance together at the door as Alex tried to open it for her. "You are a little weird, you know that?" she shouted over her shoulder as the music greeted them with an avalanche of sound.

"You'll get used to me!" Alex shouted back as he followed her in, wondering why he'd said that.

On the stage was a dark-haired dancer with more tattoos than Alex had ever seen on one person. Some of that, he realized, was because he was seeing tattoos in places you wouldn't normally see anywhere else but a strip club. *Except perhaps a bedroom*, he thought. Her makeup was all black, so was her fingernail polish, and the one part of her costume she still had on was a dog collar around her neck. In other words, a Goth.

Charlie's wrap went back in the DJ's booth and they went back to their table. Alex's beer was still there but her drink was gone.

"Want another?" he asked.

"Not right now, thanks. I'm up right after Shadow," obviously referring to the Goth girl onstage. Just as she said that, the music stopped. "My cue. See you soon," she said as she swished her way back onto the stage.

Charlie's performance wasn't a repeat of her last set. Her music was different, along with some moves on the pole that made Alex wince as he watched. *She's sure as hell a lot more flexible than I am. Then again, she does this every day, and she's about fifteen years younger than I am!*

While she performed, Alex noticed a few dancers with men in tow entering and leaving the VIP room, and he decided to ask her about that when she got back.

When she finished, she came back to the table, but just gave him a quick "I need to change, be right back" and left. She headed for the dressing room but stopped and had a word with Tanya, the older dancer Alex had watched earlier. They both glanced over at him, and after Charlie went on her way, Tanya came over to Alex's table carrying a bottle of water.

After introductions, she told him, "Charlie asked me to come and keep you company until she gets back. That way you won't have anybody else bothering you." Tanya refused his offer of something from the bar, waving her water bottle as evidence.

As they talked, Alex was amazed to learn she had three children at home and had been dancing for almost fifteen years. "It's hard to believe three kids with your body," he told her. "Impressive."

"Thank you, darling. The job helps, and I work out too. But I want to know about you. I can't remember the last time Charlie asked me to look after one of her customers. What's the deal with you two?"

Alex shrugged and replied, "We just met today. I say please and thank-you, and I open doors for ladies. I guess that makes me a little strange, especially around here."

Tanya laughed and gave him a push. "Darling, around here that makes you beyond belief! At the very least, she's going to want to find out if you're for real or just another one of *those guys*, you know?"

Alex gave Tanya a bewildered look. "'One of those guys'?" he asked her. "What does that mean?"

"Darling, you are an innocent. There are always guys who want to notch up a date with dancers like us. Some of us have stalkers, guys who get jealous if *their* girl gives another guy a dance or goes into the VIP room with them. It's our worst nightmare."

Alex was getting uncomfortable being analyzed like this, but just as he was going to reply, Charlie came back to the table. Her new costume was an orange swimming wrap thing with a cowl neckline that hid very little. As he stood up, Charlie laughed and said, "It must be a reflex! Thanks for looking after him, Tanya."

"You're welcome, sweetie. Have fun." And she was gone.

They sat down and Alex complimented her on her dancing. "Those were some wicked moves," he told her. "I'd break my back if I tried anything like that."

Charlie laughed and responded, "I haven't broken anything, but I've done other damage, believe me."

Alex decided to go for broke and ask her about the VIP room. "What's the deal with the private room? What's it like?"

"Well," she said, "there are a bunch of booths back there with sheer curtains for a little added privacy. Like I told you, you can get three dances for one hundred dollars, and then there are the champagne specials."

Alex raised his eyebrows in query and she went on.

"You pick a bottle of champagne from the list and decide on a half hour or an hour with the girl. Then we go back and have a good time. It's a hundred fifty dollars or three hundred plus the bottle."

Alex knew he didn't have that kind of cash with him, and his disappointment must have showed. He told her he wasn't prepared for that kind of outlay.

"No problem," she told him. "They take credit cards, but there's a 10 percent surcharge. Do you want to give it a try?"

It only took a moment for Alex to decide. "Sure. It's my first real night out in months. Let's go for an hour."

They stood up. Charlie took his hand, making a chill run up his arm even though her soft hand was warm in his. She led him to the other side of the room where she stopped to tell him she had to let the manager know. He replied that he needed a pit stop and headed for the restroom.

When he got back from recycling the beer, she was waiting at the entrance to the VIP room. Once again, she took his hand and led him in.

Inside the room, it was even darker than in the main club. Dim, colored bulbs lit up each of the booths. There was one back in the far corner, a little removed from the rest, and this was where she guided him.

After they'd sat down, Alanna appeared with a list and they picked out a bottle. The prices, of course, were sky-high. Alex demurred from the Dom Perignon but he didn't insist on the cheapest bottle either. He handed over his credit card to Alanna, along with a big tip, and she went off to take care of their order.

Well, one good thing about being back here is that we don't have to shout just to make ourselves heard, Alex thought.

Alanna was back in short order with a bucket full of ice and their bottle of bubbly. She put two flutes on the table and poured the wine for them. She asked if there was anything else she could get them, received their shaken negatives in return, and went bouncing off.

Suddenly feeling shy, Alex temporized by saying, "She's a cute kid."

"Yes, she is," answered Charlie as she picked up the glasses and handed one to Alex. "Cheers!" she said as she clinked her glass to his.

"That's the Way I Like It" started up. Charlie slipped off her platforms, stood up in front of Alex, and started to dance. This close, he could smell her perfume, a brand he didn't recognize, but it suited her. He could now see that she had a few tattoos scattered about her arms and back, all black. She took his hands and put them on her waist, then turned around and bent over so he could get a good view of her long legs and her tight backside.

As the music ended, she undid her top and let it slip down, giving him an unobstructed view. Then she curled up on the seat and picked up her drink.

"No rush," she said. "We've got the whole hour."

Wanting to make him comfortable, she tried to get a conversation going. "What do you for fun?" she asked him.

Trying really hard to look into her eyes and not stare, Alex replied, "When we're not in outage mode, I like to fly."

"Fly? Really? How great! Where from?" she asked.

"There's a little airport not far from here just off I-95: Waterford Airport. I share a plane with three other guys. What do you do when you're not working here or studying?"

"I like to read," Charlie said. "Lots of different kinds of stuff. Harry Potter, mysteries, Shakespeare."

"Really?" Alex interrupted. What's your favorite play?"

"*Romeo and Juliet*," she told him.

Alex looked at her and said, "I know it well." He started to recite.

> But, soft! what light through yonder window breaks?
> It is the east, and Juliet is the sun.
> Arise, fair sun, and kill the envious moon,
> Who is already sick and pale with grief,
> That thou her maid art far more fair than she:
> Be not her maid, since she is envious;
> Her vestal livery is but sick and green
> And none but fools do wear it; cast it off.
> It is my lady, O, it is my love!
> O, that she knew she were!
> She speaks yet she says nothing: what of that?
> Her eye discourses; I will answer it.
> I am too bold, 'tis not to me she speaks:
> Two of the fairest stars in all the heaven,
> Having some business, do entreat her eyes
> To twinkle in their spheres till they return.
> What if her eyes were there, they in her head?
> The brightness of her cheek would shame those stars,
> As daylight doth a lamp; her eyes in heaven
> Would through the airy region stream so bright
> That birds would sing and think it were not night.

See, how she leans her cheek upon her hand!
O, that I were a glove upon that hand,
That I might touch that cheek!

As he spoke, Charlie literally rocked back onto her heels. After the first stanza, she started mouthing the words along with him. As he finished the verse, Alex reached up and touched her cheek and was shocked to find it damp. The music started again, but instead of getting up, Charlie leaned forward and gave him a light, fleeting kiss. Then she put her lips to his ear and spoke.

"Nobody has ever, *ever* quoted Shakespeare to me back here. Alex, I have this funny feeling we are going to be very good friends."

She pulled back so he could see her face. "Does that mean you've decided I'm not *one of those guys*?" he asked her.

Charlie gave him another of those brilliant smiles. "I'll bet my ass on that," she said. "But we'll just have to find out, won't we? Oh, just so you know, I have a license to carry, and there's a Snake Slayer double-barreled pistol loaded with .410 double-aught in my purse."

"Why does that not surprise me?" Alex responded. "Well, what shall we do for the rest our time? Would you like hear some *Twelfth Night?* That's my favorite."

Charlie didn't answer. Instead, she stood up and let her outfit drop to the floor. Very few words were spoken for the rest of the hour.

CHAPTER 7

THE FOLLOWING WEEK WAS A BIT of a blur for Alex. He went to work, got his reports out, and dealt with problems as they arose, but he did it all pretty much on autopilot. If anybody at work noticed his distraction, he was oblivious to it and they said nothing.

There was one exception, however, to business as usual. The re-rack building was causing him more trouble than the rest of Trippler's projects put together. The cost-trend analysis he'd promised to run for Walker was showing them going way over budget. *It's the project from hell,* he ruminated, looking at the numbers from his latest run.

It was late on a Wednesday afternoon during the last week of February. After checking his numbers one last time, Alex decided he had to go talk to Walker. He sent the graph and table of the latest results to the printer next to his desk. When they popped out, he picked them up and headed for Walker's office.

Walker's door was closed when Alex got there, and he was obviously on the phone. Alex stood there listening to the one-sided conversation. Walker was forcefully telling the person on the other end that this BS had to stop and that he would be bucking the problem up the management chain.

When he heard the phone slam down, Alex knocked on the door and got an angry "Come in!" in response.

Alex opened the door and saw, as he expected, a very pissed-off expression on Walker's face.

"What do you want?" Walker demanded, using a tone Alex had never heard from him.

"I just finished running the latest trend analysis on the re-rack building," Alex told him from the doorway, not daring to come inside.

If anything, Walker's pissed-off attitude seemed to increase when he heard that. He waved Alex into the office and issued a firm order. "Shut the goddamn door and sit down!"

Alex did just that and handed over the results for Walker's inspection. Walker glanced at the chart, looked at the figures, threw them down on his desk, and slammed a hand down on top of the pages.

"This mother-fucking job has been a pain in my ass from day one!" he exploded. Then he seemed to struggle to get a grip on his emotions and go on in a calmer tone.

"I know this isn't your fault," he told Alex. "It's not the project supervisors' either. I know who's been throwing a wrench into the works, and it's going to stop right goddamn now. If you don't start seeing changes, especially cost reversals, coming through in the next couple of days, let me know. You got that?" Walker demanded.

"Absolutely." Alex felt he had to ask, "Who's been mucking up the job, boss?" he inquired in a tentative tone.

"None of your concern right now," Walker shot back. "You just watch the numbers and keep the updates coming. Now bug out. I have work to do."

Alex had never been so peremptorily dismissed by his boss and got up to leave. When he reached for the reports, Walker literally snarled, "I want the hard copies." Then he grabbed them off the desk and stuffed them into a drawer.

Alex went back to his desk and spent the rest of the afternoon dealing with problems in a detached, mechanical fashion. He couldn't get his mind off Walker's outburst, and he couldn't help but wonder who Walker believed was the source of their troubles.

Quitting time finally arrived, and Alex cleaned up his desk and headed out. As was frequently the case these days, when he left the plant, he headed for Rosie's to see Charlie rather than head directly home.

They still didn't have any contact outside of the club. Alex figured that it was all part of the vetting process and it would happen when it happened … or not. There didn't seem to be much he could do except keep on being himself and not push. Meanwhile, he was enjoying the company.

Every evening that week he spent an hour or two at the club with Charlie. His finances didn't allow repeats of that VIP room session, but he did indulge in a couple of "three-fers"—the three dance sets in the VIP room Charlie had told him about the night they met.

While he obviously couldn't monopolize her time (a girl has to pay her tuition), they'd talk over a drink between sets or outside when she wanted to grab a smoke.

When Charlie was dancing or occupied with another customer, Tanya, Diamond, or another of Charlie's BFFs would sit with him and keep him company. It quickly became apparent to Alex that they weren't doing this solely as a favor to Charlie. They were checking him out, trying to decide if he really was the gentleman he appeared to be or just one of those guys, one who happened to be talented at hiding his stalker alter ego.

Invariably, when his "keeper" left the table, her last words would be an admonishment to the effect of "Be good to our girl."

Alex finally brought up the subject with Charlie. "I get the feeling I must be a major topic of conversation among the ladies here," he told her. "Am I right?"

Charlie laughed and said, "Is it that obvious? Yes, everybody wants to know if you're for real. It freaks them out how you don't seem to get jealous if I spend time with another customer. And they can't figure out why such a nice guy would end up divorced."

Well that had to come up sooner or later. I was hoping for later.

"As is usually the case," he said, "it wasn't just one thing. I really don't want to go into the details just yet. Basically, it turned out we weren't as compatible as we thought. Being together got to be toxic, so we split. That's the short version, Charlie."

Charlie could see that this was a painful topic and let it pass. He changed the subject back to his inquisition. "Diamond in particular feels *very* protective of me," she told him. "We started here about the same time and we've always watched out for each other."

Happy for the distraction from his divorce, Alex told her, "That's good to know. Now I have the best friend and the den mother identified and know who to suck up to. Thank you." That got him a chuckle.

At that moment, Alex, for the first time, saw somebody he knew walk into the club. The shock registered on his face and Charlie asked what was wrong.

Leaning close, he told her, "See the older guy with the flattop haircut? His name is Frank Spencer. He's a project manager for Yankee Power. I work with him all the time. He's the last person I ever expected to see here!"

"Really? Why? And you really didn't know that he and Sparkle have a thing going?"

Alex sat back in his chair, dumbfounded. "You have got to be kidding me!" he exclaimed. "He is one of the most miserable people on the face of the Earth. He walks around mad all the time, ready to blow a gasket at the slightest provocation. I don't know why anybody would want to spend time with him."

Charlie got a very serious, perhaps even conspiratorial look on her face. She leaned close again and said, "Their relationship isn't like ours. It's more commercial, if you get my meaning."

Alex's astonishment meter was ready to peg out. "She's not taking money to sleep with him, is she?"

Charlie thought for a moment before replying. "I don't think it's as simple as that. He comes in pretty often. He gives her a lot of nice presents—jewelry and other stuff. I think he tips her some large ones to help with the rent, but he never flashes the cash here. Short answer? No, I don't think she's sleeping with him just for money."

Alex shook his head and tried to wrap his mind around Frank Spencer with a dancer girlfriend. *Hell I have one, sort of. He's just as entitled.*

Spencer walked right up to the stage where Sparkle was dancing. As soon as she spotted him, she gave out a squeal of delight, kneeled down on the stage, and hugged him around the neck. It was, Alex realized, the first time he had ever seen Frank Spencer smile. After the hug, he spoke something into her ear and her expression changed from happy to frightened.

I wonder what he just told her to get that reaction, Alex thought. Then he gave a shake of his head and turned his attention back to Charlie. She was telling him she was going to be busy with midterms for the next week. When she finished, he decided that this might be the time to try to take another step in their strange and wonderful relationship. He reached into his wallet and pulled out one of his business cards, then took a pen from his pocket and wrote down his personal e-mail address and his cell number. He pushed it over to her.

"Why don't you drop me an e-mail or call me when you know what your schedule's going to be? If I come by when you're not here, or call, that might get a stalker rep going. That doesn't seem like a good idea."

Charlie looked down at the card then up at Alex. "That's a big move, sweetie. I'm not sure I'm ready for that."

Alex told her, "It can be one-way for now. Set up a Gmail or AOL account to use just for us. Block your cell number if you call. It doesn't have to be a problem for you, really."

Alex could actually see her thoughts play out on her face. *She's a great dancer, and she'll probably be a great criminologist, but I bet she's a lousy poker player.*

Finally, she said, "Okay, you're right. I'll set up an account tonight after I get back to the dorm and send you an e-mail. Once again, you've managed to surprise me. Thank you." Her last words were accompanied by a peck on the cheek, an act just inside the house rules.

After that, Alex decided to not stay much longer. That big step had a put a momentary strain on the relationship and he decided it might be good to give Charlie a little space. He stayed until her next set started and said good-night. Then he drove home, hoping he hadn't messed things up.

The thought stayed with him as he fixed dinner and watched a WWII flick on TCM. It was still there when he climbed in between his cold sheets and haunted him for quite a while in the darkness. *C'mon Alex,* he told himself, *the deed is done. The quicker you go to sleep, the quicker the morning will be here and you'll know if you've scared her off or not.* Sometime in the small, dark hours of the night, he finally fell asleep.

The next thing he knew, there was some distant ringing that wouldn't go away. He finally pulled himself out of the depths of sleep to realize it was his cell phone, sitting on the nightstand. More than half-asleep, he fumbled for the phone, found the answer button, and put the phone to his ear.

"Hello, who is it? What do you want?" he mumbled.

"Alex!" The panic and fear in that just that one word forced him into wakefulness.

"Who's this? What's wrong?" he demanded. The fear in heart was that something had happened to Charlie.

"Alex, it's Patricia! You need to get into the office right away!"

"Patricia," he told her, "calm down. What's the problem? What's happened?" Alex couldn't imagine anything that would justify a call like this. Even if one of the reactor cores was melting down, the problem would be handled by YP, not Trippler.

He could hear Patricia taking a deep breath, then in a voice that sounded like it was close to tears, she told him, "Walker James is dead! Big Mike told me to call all the staff in to be questioned by the police. The cleaning people found him just a little while ago. Alex, this is just awful!"

Sitting up and already reaching for clothes, Alex told her, "Okay, Patricia, okay. I'm only a few miles from the plant and I'll be there in ten or fifteen minutes, max. Take a deep breath and make the rest of your calls, and let whoever is in charge there know that I'm on my way in."

CHAPTER **8**

ALEX'S ESTIMATE WOULD HAVE BEEN GOOD if it hadn't been for the Waterford PD cruiser blocking the access road. The cop manning it didn't want to believe that Alex had actually been called in, and it took him a good ten minutes to get somebody inside the fence to confirm Alex was wanted at the Trippler offices, like yesterday.

When he got to the MAP, there were even more WPD cars with their blinking blue lights pulled right up against the end of the parking lot. There was also a van from the OCME, the medical examiner. Seeing that was a fist in the gut. Alex found the first spot available and went through the routine of entering the plant proper.

Another uniformed officer standing guard at the entrance to the Trippler offices put him through the wringer again. When he finally got inside, the place was a madhouse. Cops were directing all Trippler personnel into the project supervisor's bullpen. The cop keeping an eye on them asked his name, checked his badge, and then checked him off a list. He told him to stay in the area, that detectives were taking statements and he'd be called when it was his turn.

The talk in the bullpen wasn't about Walker's death. It was grousing about being kept away from the coffee. It was noisy but really not all that crowded, which made sense since most of the people who worked for Trippler lived much farther away than he did. Many of them had an hour-long drive, some even more.

Alex cooled his heels for about twenty minutes before being called into Big Mike's office. Sitting behind Mike's desk was a stocky man in a dark suit. He looked tired and unhappy, probably not pleased with being called out at five on a cold February morning.

He stood up and introduced himself as Detective Joel Samms of the WPD, at which point the door opened and a taller, red-haired man in a gray suit entered unannounced. From the look on Samms face, Alex could tell he wasn't happy to see the newcomer.

"Special Agent Harkness. What a pleasant surprise. And what brings the FBI here so early in the morning?" Samms' tone made it very clear he was not pleased to see the FBI man.

"Hello, Samms," the FBI agent replied. "I know your department has jurisdiction, but because it's a nuclear facility, we have to be involved in the investigation too. Sorry, but that's the way it is."

Samms gave a loud sniff and waved Harkness to another chair. Alex could tell the detective knew this was a fight he would not win.

"Agent Harkness, allow me to introduce Mr. Alex Strong. He is an employee of Trippler Power and, if my information is correct, the deceased was his supervisor. Is that correct, Mr. Strong?"

"Yes, sir, it is," Alex replied.

"And do you know anything surrounding the circumstances of Mr. James' death?" the detective continued.

"No, I do not. The first I knew of it was the call I got this morning telling me to report in. I would have been here sooner but it took me ten minutes to get past your car at the access road."

"I'm glad to hear they're doing their job, sir. Now tell me: what is your position here?"

"I'm a cost analyst and computer support person. I generate the reports Walker uses." He paused. "*Used* to use to manage our projects," Alex told him.

"When was the last time you saw Mr. James?" the detective went on.

"Yesterday, about 4:00 PM. Excuse me, please," Alex said as he reached for his phone when it suddenly sounded off.

"No calls," the FBI man jumped in.

"I'm not going to answer it," Alex shot back, matching the agent's glare. "Just send it to voice mail and shut it off, if that's okay with you?"

"Sure, sure," said the WPD man. "Thank you. Please tell me about the last time you saw Mr. James."

Alex told them about the loud telephone conversation Walker had had as he stood outside the door. Then he related his discussion with Walker about the project overrun. When he finished, the detective looked at his notepad with an expression like he'd just bitten into something sour. "You say Mr. James put the printouts in his desk?" he asked.

"That's right," Alex replied.

"I have the inventory of his desk here," Samms told him. "Nothing like that is listed."

Alex shrugged his shoulders and replied, "I saw him put them there. I have no idea what happened to them after that."

"Can you reproduce the reports?" broke in the FBI agent, earning himself a look from the local detective.

"Certainly, as long as the data are still there in my computer. I haven't been allowed access to my work area. Even if that were gone, I could reconstruct the data from the corporate mainframe in an hour or so."

"What makes you think your computer or the data might not be there?" came the question from Samms.

"You're investigating a death. I know nothing about the circumstances, but it is conceivable that if somebody murdered Walker, he or she might also try and tamper with records besides the ones taken from his desk. If not that, it's also conceivable that you might take the office computers into evidence for examination. Am I wrong?" he asked, looking back and forth between the two lawmen.

Samms and Harkness exchanged looks and ignored his question. Samms resumed. "Where were you after you left work last night?"

"After I left the plant, I went to Rosie's, over on the bay. I was there until about seven thirty. After that, I went home and was there until I got the call this morning."

"Anybody who can confirm that?" asked Samms.

"I'm something of a regular at Rosie's. You can confirm with a dancer named Charlie and several of her friends. I left alone and was home alone all night."

Samms made notes and then asked, "What's Charlie's last name?"

"I don't know," Alex replied. "We aren't that close. I don't even know if that's her real name."

"And nobody can confirm you were at home?" Samms pushed.

"My landlord or his wife may have heard me come in, but you can surely confirm I wasn't here," Alex pushed back. "The security system will show exactly when I exited the site and that I didn't come back until this morning. Actually, that's true for everybody who works here."

At that point, a light bulb went off in Alex's head. "That's your problem, isn't it?" he asked the LEOs while swinging his head back and forth to see their reaction. "I bet everybody who could possibly have killed Walker is accounted for by the security system. What you have is the biggest locked-room mystery in history! What's your theory?"

The two cops looked at each other again, and then Harkness answered. "Smart fellow, aren't you? Smart enough to beat security?"

Alex shook his head and replied, "I have no reason to. I had no problems with Walker. Just the opposite. I'm sure you'll look at all the performance reviews and find he gave me top marks. I told you about the one project that has been giving us trouble since day one. Walker said it wasn't my fault, or the fault of the project supervisors, that it was such a mess. If it wasn't us, the next logical person to look at would be the project manager from Yankee Power. His name is Frank Spencer. Have you talked to him yet?"

"We'll get to everybody in their turn, Mr. Strong," came the cool response from Samms. "And you're jumping to a conclusion that this was a murder. As of now, it's merely an unattended death. It wouldn't be getting anywhere near this much attention if it weren't for the fact it took place inside the fence here at Osprey Point."

Samms paused and glared before continuing. "You are correct that we will be looking at your computer and some others. Once we're done with that, we may ask you to recreate the report you ran for Mr. James. Oh, if you would be so kind as to provide us with your password, that would be a big help."

Samms handed him a pad and a pencil and Alex wrote down his regular user name and password. *If they want the admin credentials, let them ask for them,* he thought.

"That will be all for now. We know how to get in touch if we need you. Check with your site manager, but I expect you will have the day off. Thank you. You can go now."

He gestured toward the door. Alex got up, unwilling to leave without more information, but it was obvious he would get nothing more from these two, so he turned and left. Behind him, he heard Samms call out, "Sergeant! Next person!"

The officer outside the door pointed toward the accounting area. *Evidently, they're keeping those who have made statements apart from those who haven't. If they had enough room, they'd probably have us isolated. Just what the hell is going on? What happened to Walker?*

In the accounting area, he found Big Mike and several other Trippler employees. They were all looking much more upset than the people in the bullpen. It was as if talking to the detective brought home the fact that one of their own was dead. Unlike the rowdiness of the bullpen, the tone here was subdued. Some people were talking quietly; others were just sitting and staring.

One of the people in the room was Patricia, his field accountant friend who had called him, unbelievably, less than two hours ago. She was sitting in a chair and sniffling when he came in. When she saw him, she got up, ran over to him, and gave him a hug while her crying picked up.

"How could this happen?" she blubbered. "I saw him yesterday. He was fine!" And then she dissolved into tears again. Alex tried to comfort her, and after a couple of minutes, she did quiet down.

Then Alex saw Big Mike motion him over.

"All done, Alex? If they've finished with you, you can go home. There's nothing you can do here today. Probably not tomorrow either. Eight hours pay today and tomorrow. Plan on being back on Monday. The cops are keeping the accountants until everybody's been notified and the police have finished their interviews, but you can go."

"What the hell happened?" Alex asked his boss. "They're not saying anything about how Walker died!"

Big Mike shook his big mane of salt-and-pepper hair and replied, "I don't know, Alex; I just don't know. I'm afraid they may be thinking it's a suicide."

Big Mike's words rocked Alex back on his heels. "I don't believe it! I started out as a psychologist, Mike. I did my time on suicide prevention hotlines and rotations on psych units. There's no way in *hell* Walker killed himself!"

Mike listened to Alex's outburst and replied, "That may well be, son. We just don't know yet." He reached out and shook Alex's shoulder. "Go home, take the time off, and we'll see what happens on Monday. Sock in some supplies on the way. There's supposed to be a big late-season storm moving in tonight."

After giving Patricia another hug, Alex left the trailer and started the long trek back to his truck. Just before reaching the MAP, he remembered the call that came in while he was being interviewed and realized his phone was still off. He switched it on, saw that he had a voice mail waiting, and punched up his mailbox.

The electronic voice told him the message was from a blocked number. He frowned and almost hit the delete button, but then he remembered what Charlie and he had talked about last night and hit play instead. Sure enough, Charlie's voice came through the speaker.

"Hi, Alex," she said. "I kept my promise. You should find an e-mail waiting for you with an address to use. Let me know if you got it. I'm working tonight but not tomorrow or the weekend. Bye bye, sweetie."

Even as he hit delete, his phone vibrated to an incoming e-mail. Sure enough, along with a half-dozen other messages he hadn't had time to look at this morning, there was one from charliethedancer@gmail.com. *Well, I shouldn't have any trouble remembering that.* The message itself was a one-liner, and he decided not to answer it until he got home.

Instead of making his usual trek to the Stop & Shop over the bridge in Groton (a move designed to keep from running into his ex), Alex made a quick stop at the IGA in East Lyme to pick up food for the weekend, then he stopped and filled up the truck and made sure his washer fluid was topped off. Next, he swung past Waterford Airport to make sure his plane was safely tucked into its hangar before the storm hit.

But despite the busy work, the mystery of Walker's death kept running through his mind. *How did he die? When? Nobody's calling it an accident, which they would if they could. That leaves murder or suicide. Which is it?*

I don't believe suicide, so that leaves murder. Who and why? Spencer? Who else could it be?

Satisfied that he was as ready as he could be for the storm, he headed home, the same questions rolling through his mind again and again with no answers to be found. He got home, put away the stuff that needed to go in the refrigerator, and then typed an e-mail to Charlie. "Got ur call & email. Big trouble @ work. Pls call ASAP." After sending it, he put away the rest of his groceries and cleaned up the rest of his e-mail. *You're going to have a long, cold weekend, Alex. What the hell am I going to do here for four days?*

CHAPTER 9

ALEX SPENT HALF AN HOUR SURFING cable channels, trying to block out the events of the day. He found himself checking The Weather Channel every ten minutes for updates on the storm, wishing and waiting for Charlie to call him back. He was about to turn off the TV and go make lunch when he spotted a shot of the Point on the screen. He quickly clicked back to the channel to hear what the news anchor was saying.

"Authorities are investigating the death of a man employed by the maintenance contractor at Osprey Point Nuclear Generating Station in Waterford. Both local police and FBI are involved in the investigation. So far, all News5 has learned for certain is the name of the deceased, Walker James, and that he was an employee of Trippler Power. Authorities are refusing to speculate on the cause of death until an autopsy has been completed by the Office of the Chief Medical Examiner. However, there are unconfirmed reports the death may be drug related. We will continue to follow the story and inform you of any new developments."

Alex stared at the screen, dumbfounded. *Drugs? Drugs! No fucking way! Between the pre-employment screening and the random checks they do on us, there's no way that can be true! Only an idiot would believe something like that!*

Alex was still fuming about the story and ranting to himself when the phone rang. He grabbed it from the arm of his chair before the second ring could finish and didn't even check the caller ID. He almost shouted, "Hello!" into the phone.

Charlie's voice, anxious and concerned, came out the speaker. "Alex, I got your e-mail. What's wrong, sweetie? You sound really upset."

Alex took a deep breath and got himself under control before he answered. "Charlie, I know I've mentioned my boss, Walker James. Do you remember?"

"Sure, I remember. Why?"

"He's dead, Charlie. His body was found in his office this morning." Alex heard her gasp but kept right on. "There's no way it was an accident. Our site manager said he thinks the cops are going for suicide, but that makes no sense to me. There was nothing in his behavior pointing to that. It was just on the news that it may have been drug related, but that's impossible to swallow, too."

"Honey, I know you're upset, but why is that impossible? I'm not trying to change your mind. I just want to know why you think so."

"Charlie, everybody at the Point goes through pre-employment drug screening. We also get tested randomly a couple of times a year. One strike and you're out; zero tolerance. You just can't have people high on anything working around nukes. The risks are too great. I think they're trying to scapegoat Walker, and Trippler too for that matter. The only alternative is that he was murdered."

"Murdered?" asked Charlie, her tone incredulous. "That's a big jump, Alex. How could that be?"

"I don't know," he admitted. "The problem is the security system. It keeps track of everybody going in and out of the plant and to some extent their movements inside. I realized that while a local detective and an FBI man were interviewing me this morning. It's a locked-room mystery right out of Sherlock Holmes, only the room is five hundred acres big."

Charlie was silent as she digested what Alex had told her, and then she asked, "Was OCME there, the medical examiner?"

"Yeah, I saw their van by the access point and one of their people waiting with the gurney in our building. I guess the body hadn't been removed yet."

"Alex, I need you to think about the person with the gurney. Did you see an ID? Man or woman? Give me a description."

The strange request took Alex by surprise and he didn't argue. "I have to think," he told her. "Let me replay the whole walk in. Give me a minute."

Alex closed his eyes, held the phone up against his chest, and started to walk through the whole episode from the time he reached the MAP. He wasn't sure how long it took to get to the point where he entered Trippler's offices, but once he got there, the pay-off was immediate.

He put the phone back to his ear. "It was a man," he told Charlie. "I didn't see an ID or his face, but he was tall, skinny, and had red hair. What difference does it make?"

"What it does is give me an 'in' on the autopsy. That's Alan Tipton. He's an assistant in the OCME's office and usually covers this area."

"And you know this how?" demanded Alex, confused by her sudden display of insider knowledge.

"He's a friend of mine. I did an internship with the Connecticut OCME last year. If you want, I can call him tonight or tomorrow and find out what the preliminary says. I doubt we'll learn anything today. They'll hardly have gotten the body back to Hartford. You said the FBI was there? And who was the local detective?"

Alex nodded at the phone and told her, "Yes, Special Agent Harkness was his name. I don't know where the nearest FBI office is, but he's probably from there. The detective's name was Samms."

"It's in New London," Charlie told him. "I only know one person in that field office, but I'll see what I can find out. Regardless, if the FBI's interested, they'll put a rush on the autopsy. I don't think I know any people in Waterford PD, but I'll see if some of my other contacts do. How's that sound for a plan?"

"Honey, you are the best. Thank you. Thanks a million. I owe you big time for this!"

"You bet your ass you do. I've got to get to class. I'll call you later."

"Thank you again, sweetheart," Alex told her. And then the recollection hit him. "Oh my God!"

"What? What?" she demanded.

"The cops will be coming to talk to you and maybe some of the other girls. You're part of my alibi for yesterday! I'm glad I remembered. It would have been a real shock to have them show up out of the blue."

"Thanks for telling me," Charlie said, and then she chuckled. "Just how detailed shall I be concerning our activities yesterday?"

Alex felt his face blush as he told her, "Just the truth, the whole truth, and nothing but the truth. I can handle it."

She laughed at him. "Okay, let me deal with it. You take care. I'll call you later. Bye, honey."

"Good-bye, Charlie. Thanks again." Then he broke the connection and started to think some more.

I'll be damned. Sometimes I forget what Charlie does when she isn't dancing! The idea she might already have contacts inside law enforcement never occurred to me. I hope she can get something useful out of that friend of hers.

His check-in with Charlie completed, Alex went back to making lunch. He had a bowl of soup in the microwave and had just started to make coffee when it came to him. *Jake! I need to call Jake!*

Pulling his phone from his pocket, he hit the speed-dial number for his old friend. It rang for a long time and Alex was already composing a voice mail message in his head when Jake answered.

"Hiya, Alex. We just got out of a briefing by the plant super about what happened. I can't tell you how sorry I am. Is there anything I can do for you?"

"No, buddy. I just wanted to touch base. Tell me: what did the super have to have to say?"

"Nothing good," was his friend's reply. "He was dropping hints about some sort of drug connection. Had you heard that?"

Alex gave a derisive snort and replied, "That's what the TV news is saying too. Now I have an idea of where they got it. You know how ridiculous that is, right?"

"Yes, I do. So does he. But it's my guess that nothing about our drug-testing program is going to make the news. Walker's going to be crucified as some kind of rogue worker who managed to slip through the cracks. The superintendent wants this swept under the rug something fierce."

"Doesn't surprise me," Alex said. "YP will probably put pressure on us to take responsibility for hiring a bad apple. Damn it, Jake, it just doesn't make sense! The only person who has access to the plant and something like a motive is Frank Spencer."

"Spencer! How the hell do you figure that? What could his motive possibly be?" his friend demanded.

Alex related the phone call he'd overheard, his discussion with Walker, and the interview he'd had that morning with the detective. "The thing that keeps coming back to me is how Walker specifically said it wasn't my fault or the fault of the project supervisors. That pretty much leaves somebody working for the client, and the most obvious person is Spencer."

Jake thought about that for a while before he answered. The words came out slowly and carefully, like he was still thinking. "Okay, I see your point. But all I can say is that we'll have to wait and see if Spencer has an alibi. One other thing we found out at the briefing was that Walker apparently died between eight and ten last night. Spencer, as far as I know, wouldn't have any reason for being in the plant at that hour, not when there's no outage running."

"Neither would Walker," replied Alex, "but he was there. The only reason I can think of is that he was going to confront in person whoever he was talking to earlier on the phone. Do you know if the phone system in the plant keeps call logs?"

"I don't think so," Jake told him. "For certain not on internal calls since they don't cost us anything. I'm not sure about outside calls."

"Well, if that call was outside, maybe they can track it. Meanwhile there's another way we might get some additional information." Alex then related his conversation with Charlie.

"Full of surprises, that girlfriend of yours," was Jake's response.

"She's not my girlfriend. Well, sort of. Maybe. How can you call somebody a girlfriend when you aren't even sure you know her real name? I realized that when I had to tell the cops about her as part of my alibi!"

"She'll certainly do for now," said Jake. "Look, I've got to go. You hang tight and I'll be in touch if I hear anything else, okay? I'll call you this evening to check in regardless."

As usual, Jake was a rock in times of trouble. "Thanks, brother. I appreciate that. I'll talk to you later." He killed the call.

Alex finished his coffee then made a sandwich to go with his soup and sat down at the kitchen table to eat. Once again, he started to replay the events of the day and his conversations with Charlie and Jake. The one thing he kept coming back to was the security system. The more he thought about it, the more he realized how little he knew about it. He slurped down his last spoonful of soup, poured another cup of coffee, and headed to his desk at the living room end of the bedroom.

He plopped down into his ragged desk chair then logged into his PC. He brought up his Deep Web browser and started doing searches on nuclear security. First, he got a false trail having to do with nuclear weapons, but before long, he was drilling for information on sites that, not too surprisingly, had to do with hacking security systems in general. He found a forum that he could access as read-only and finally hit the mother lode.

He spent the next couple hours reading threads about various systems used at US and foreign plants. The term that appeared in almost every post was WATCHDOG, a system developed by a low-profile company out in Silicon Valley named HyperSec. The more Alex read, the more he realized that this was probably the system being used at Osprey Point. The details agreed with his daily experience and the few security drills he'd witnessed. *Or they might have been real incidents. They wouldn't want to let us know, would they?*

Alex finally pushed back from his desk and stretched out his arms and legs. Shaking his head to loosen up his neck, he realized that it must have started snowing some time ago. The ground was covered with the white stuff. As he watched, he realized there were times when he could hardly see across the street. *Whew! Coming down thick and fast! I hate the reason why, but I'm glad I'm not out driving in this.*

He circled around to the kitchen for more coffee then settled back down in front of the television. As he sipped the brew, he realized that making coffee was what had prompted him to call Jake. His buddy loved coffee just a bit less than he loved his wife.

He found an old flying movie on TCM and had settled in to watch it when his phone rang. He checked the number. It wasn't coming up as somebody in his address book. He hit answer and said, "Hello?"

"Alex! It's Charlie. I'm sorry to bother you but I'm in trouble."

That got Alex's attention. He sat straight up and replied, What's wrong, honey? What's happened?" *It must be bad. She forgot to block her number!*

"I was headed to the club and slid off the road. It was stupid to even try and go in, I know. I'm okay, but I bent a wheel. A tow truck got the car, but I'm stuck at the Burger King up on Flanders Road, just south of 95. I know your truck is a 4x4 so maybe you could come and give me a ride home? Please?"

Without a moment's hesitation, Alex answered, "Of course I'll come and get you. I have no idea how long it will take, but I'll be there. Keep an eye out for me. You just stay inside where it's warm. Okay?"

The relief in her voice was palpable. "Okay. See you soon. Thank you!"

Alex grabbed his keys, coat and hat, then hit the remote starter--all in one fluid rush of motion as he headed for the door. As soon as he opened it, he realized this wasn't going to be a quick trip. The rather steep stairs were already covered in an icy mix of snow and sleet. He turned back into his apartment, grabbed a broom, and started sweeping his way down the landing and stairs.

When he got to his truck, he used the broom to clear away the snow. There was some ice on the windshield, but by the time he was done clearing all the windows and lights, the defroster was already starting to melt it. He threw the broom in the back of the truck and got in.

It was a slow and slippery trip. The roads were bad enough, but the bridge over Niantic Bay was worse. It took him twenty minutes to drive the six miles to the Burger King.

As soon as he pulled up to the door, he saw Charlie heading for the truck, carrying her big bag. Before she had a chance to open the passenger door, he flipped the seat forward so she could toss the bag into the back of the cab. He flipped it back and she climbed in, twisting in the seat to give him a hug.

"Thank you so much, sweetie! I would have been stuck there all night! People coming in were saying that the governor has closed the roads. Thank you, a thousand times, thank you."

After Alex returned her hug, he gave her a long hard look before saying, "The roads are closed? I-95 is shut down?"

"That's what they said. How will we get to Conn College?"

Alex made a decision, one that she probably wasn't going to like. "We aren't. I'm taking you home with me," he told her. "My place is closer and we don't have to get on the highway. You're coming with me. No arguments."

Charlie looked like a deer caught in the headlights. Her first response was, predictably, "I don't know if that's a good idea, Alex."

"Look," he told her, "I just stocked up on food. You can take the bed and I'll sleep on the couch. If I try anything funny, you've got your Snake Slayer. The roads are only getting worse and it just makes no sense to go farther than we have to in this weather."

She searched his eyes for several seconds before replying. "You're right, but I'm still not sure this is a good idea. But I made you come out in this and I'm not going to make you drive to my place *and* back home. Let's go."

He gave her a quick nod of agreement, put the truck in gear, and started the long crawl home.

Chapter 10

THE TRIP BACK TOOK TEN MINUTES more than the drive out. Alex noticed that Charlie kept quiet and let him drive, but he couldn't tell if her tense body language was due to the journey or the destination. Maybe both.

He was very grateful that he was going down, not up, the hill just west of his apartment. Alex went down in 4WD compound low, watching several cars struggling to go the other way, and spotted one Toyota in the weeds by the side of the road. The driver was standing in the frozen slush and talking to a Waterford PD officer in an SUV.

It took some doing to get the truck up the driveway and into the parking area in back of the house, but they made it.

Alex looked over at Charlie and started to try to defuse the tension with a joke but decided it wasn't going to work. Instead, he just cleared his throat and said, "Well, we made it. Stay there and let me get the door for you. It's slippery and I've got better boots than you do."

He didn't wait for an answer but popped the door and grabbed the broom as he went around the back of the truck to get to Charlie's door. He helped her out and then left her hanging onto the door as he reached in and grabbed her big bag. He gave it to her, saying, "Sling that over your shoulder, give me your other arm, and hold on."

She took the bag and his arm, shut the door, and turned to look at the house. Her gaze followed the long stairway leading to the attic apartment, and then she told him, "That looks kind of dangerous from here, Alex." Then she noticed the broom and continued. "You really do come prepared. Were you a Boy Scout?"

"Yes, but I never made it past Tenderfoot," he replied. "Don't worry; they were pretty clear when I left. I'll go first and sweep the snow away. Hang on to me until we get to the foot of the stairs," he told her.

The plan worked. Leaning the broom on the rail of the landing, he fumbled with his keys. He unlocked the door, gestured for her to go in first, and then followed and closed the door.

This is the first time I've had two people in this kitchen, he thought. *It's tight in here!*

Charlie, of course, gave the place her trained X-ray once-over then turned to him and asked, "Where should I put my stuff?"

"Sit down first and get out of your boots." He pulled a kitchen chair up for her, shrugged out of his own coat, and then took her boots. He put them against the wall and added his own. Then he took her coat and hung both of them in the small closet next to the bathroom.

"Okay, time for the grand tour," he said as he turned and stood in front of the closet. "The bathroom's right here," he told her, pointing across the hallway. "There's a RON kit you can use under the sink. It's in a clear plastic pouch with pink trim."

"A RON kit?" she asked. "What's that?"

"Sorry. That means **R**emain **O**ver **N**ight. It's a term pilots use, usually when they're stuck somewhere they didn't intend to be. We keep a guy version in the plane. I keep a ladies version around too. It's got a toothbrush, toothpaste, soap, and uh, other things you might need."

"Alex, you're blushing. And you were a married man?"

Ignoring her teasing, Alex took her bag and headed to the bedroom through the kitchen. "Bedroom's here. I'll get clean sheets on for you before bedtime." He put the bag on the floor, opened his dresser, and pulled out a towel, washcloth, and sheets that he put on top of the dresser. "The closet is right there, if you want to hang up anything."

Charlie had followed behind him and poked her head into the bedroom to look around. She saw it ran the full depth of the apartment from front to back, saw the desk at the other end, then noticed two odd things about the bed. The first was that it was neatly made but obviously slept in. "Alex, do you really make your bed every day? And the bed goes from wall to wall. How in the world do you make it up?"

Ignoring the first question, Alex laughed and replied, "You'll see! Believe me: it will be a whole lot easier to do with two of us!" Then he backed them out to the kitchen, showed her where things like glasses and cups were located, and reversed again to lead her into the living room.

"Sit down and take it easy. Can I get you anything? Coffee, tea? I've got Earl Grey and chamomile. Chamomile would be good for your nerves."

As she curled up on the couch, Charlie told him, "I think you need it more than I do, but I'll have a cup. Alex, relax. You got us here in one piece, right?" She let loose one of her dazzling smiles and added, "Plus, I still have my Snake Slayer!"

Alex gave her a rueful grin in reply, handed her the remote, and went out in the kitchen to get water boiling. As he got tea things together, he heard her flipping channels. Somehow, he wasn't surprised when she stopped on The Weather Channel. The forecaster was talking about the nor'easter, and none of it sounded good.

"When do you have to go back to work?" Charlie shouted from the living room.

"Probably not until Monday!" Alex called back. Then he walked the few steps to the living room entrance and continued. "Our site manager said that we'd for sure have today off and probably tomorrow because of the investigation. Add the storm into the equation, and it's pretty certain we'll be out until Monday. Jeez, I can't remember the last time I had four days off in a row. It must be a couple of years."

In a sympathetic tone, Charlie told him, "I wish the reason why wasn't so bad, really I do."

Alex was saved from answering by the teapot whistling. He went back and poured boiling water into two mugs then called out, "Milk? Sugar?" and Charlie replied, "Nothing."

Balancing the two mugs on a plate (along with milk and sweeteners— just in case), he carried them in and laid them down on the coffee table. He joined Charlie on the couch but was careful to scrunch himself into the corner opposite her, something she instantly noticed.

"Alex, it was your idea to bring me here to wait out the storm. Will you please relax? Come on, honey. Quit treating me like I'm contagious. I promise I won't shoot you without warning."

It is hard to imagine that cute little lady killing me in cold blood. Okay, Alex, settle down and take it easy.

With a sheepish grin, Alex spread out a bit from the corner of the couch and told her, "You're right. I'm sorry. Believe it or not, you're the first visitor I've had since I moved in six months ago."

"You must be kidding. Did she really hurt you that bad?"

The reference to his ex-wife took Alex by surprise. He nodded then said, "The first few months were pretty bad, but once I got settled in here and work got busy, it got better. I managed to get some flying in before the weather got too crummy and that helped, too."

Charlie looked around the living room and commented, "You don't look all that settled, sweetie. I don't see much here that looks like it belongs to you."

Another nod. "Right. Most of my stuff is in storage. I left stuff packed up because I'm hoping to find a job out of the area, but no bites, yet. It's hard to look when you're working sixty-hour weeks. But there's a bookshelf in the headboard you couldn't see and another on the far side of the desk, so I have my old favorites with me. Plus the library is right down the street. There's a picture of the airplane on my desk too. Want to see?"

"Of course. It's so cool that you really own an airplane. Will you take me flying someday?"

"Say the word," he told her as he went to get the framed eight-by-ten. "There she is. Give her gas and oil and a little TLC and she never complains. And she always brings me back in one piece."

He sat down on the couch, closer to Charlie this time, and handed her the picture. Charlie looked at it and saw a sleek red, white, and blue airplane. She hadn't seen many little airplanes up close, but this didn't look like any of them. "What is it?" she asked.

"It's a Cessna Cardinal," Alex told her. "You can tell because it doesn't have any wing struts. Compared to other Cessnas, there weren't a lot of them built."

"It's pretty! How long have you owned it?"

"About ten years, but I don't own all of it. It's a four-way partnership."

"It must cost a fortune," she remarked.

"You don't fly because it's cheap," he admitted. "There's more to it than just getting from A to B. A lot of people, me included, think there's a very spiritual aspect to flying."

Just then, Charlie's phone rang. She took one look at it and said, "It's Alan." Then she answered the call.

Instantly, Alex's tension was back. He wished she could put it on speaker, but he knew that wasn't a good idea. The call, however, didn't last long.

"Alan was just letting me know they got held up by the storm. He probably won't be able to tell me anything until tomorrow afternoon. I'm sorry."

"Sorry for what? You're trying to help me deal with this and that makes you number one on a very short list. No, don't think it for a moment."

Their happy mood had been broken by the phone call and Alex was trying to find a way to get it back. "What would you like to do about dinner?" he asked her. "I can't do anything fancy, but we can do spaghetti, a chicken stir-fry, or maybe cacciatore? That's a specialty of mine. I've got some decent Australian wine to go with it. Red or white? Take your pick. How's that sound?"

"You cook? You have got be kidding me. Who taught you?"

"My mother, some. My dad cooked too. I learned a lot from cookbooks and cooking shows, but this cacciatore recipe belongs to my mother."

"This I've got to see," Charlie declared. "Can I help?"

"Nope, the cooking is my job. This takes a while to do right, so let me get started, get the wine chilling, and then we'll try and find a movie to watch or something."

Alex went to the kitchen and started the prep work. While he was working, he heard Charlie on her phone, telling someone, evidently her roommate, that she'd been caught in the storm, was spending the night at a friend's house, and not to worry. Then she placed another call, this one obviously to her mother, to reassure her and see how her parents were weathering the storm. That one took a while. After she finished, she called out, "Mind if I look at your library?"

"Go ahead!" he shouted back as he got the last of the ingredients into the pot. He covered it and set it on simmer, then went back into the living room.

Charlie was curled up back on the couch, a John Grisham mystery in her hands. She looked up as he came in and said, "That smells freaking awesome. I guess you can cook."

Alex smiled and told her, "Tell me that after you taste it. More tea? Just want to read?"

Charlie put the book down and gave him a very serious look. "What about you? Do you want to talk about any of this?"

Alex shook his head. "Just about anything else but. Tell you what, if you don't mind, let's get the sheets changed. That way, we won't have to worry about it later."

"Okay, this I've gotta see."

"You stay on this side," Alex told her. "I'll go around the other."

He circled through the kitchen and entered the bedroom from the other door. He started pulling off the blankets and sheets, Charlie helping to get the far corners of the bottom sheet loose. Then he tossed her the clean bottom sheet and asked her to hook the corner on.

"How *do* you do this by yourself?" she demanded. "Hop back and forth over the bed?"

Alex laughed and told her, "I tried, but it messes it up too much. No, I end up running around the apartment four or five times getting everything snugged down. I'm sure you'd get a good laugh out of watching me!"

"Oh, I'd give a night's tips to see that. Other than that, it is a cute little apartment."

"Yeah, I was lucky," Alex replied. "I had noticed the for-rent sign a couple times before the blowup. When I had to move out, I came by and it was still there."

When they finished, he folded up the used sheets and put them aside for his use later on, then he turned around and they rendezvoused back in the living room.

This time as they settled down, Charlie gave him a long, searching look then said, "You look beat, sweetie. Why don't you lie down and take a nap? I'll take the chair so you can stretch out. Grisham can keep me company."

Suddenly, Alex felt very tired. He bowed to her judgment and retrieved a pillow from the bedroom. Before settling down, he asked her, "Can you please watch the chicken? It needs to stay on a low simmer. Just give it a stir once in a while. Wake me up about six?"

Charlie stood up to give him room to lie down. After he stretched out, she gave him a peck on the forehead and said, "Don't worry. I'll keep an eye on it. Go to sleep."

With that, Alex closed his eyes and with one last thought of *why* and *who,* he drifted off.

It seemed like he had only closed his eyes when he felt a hand on his shoulder and Charlie's voice in his ear. "Alex, wake up. It's six o'clock. Wake up, sweetie!"

He half-rolled and saw her silhouetted against the window, which was showing only a dim, gray light. "You snore. Did you know that?" she asked.

Stretching himself and shaking his head to clear it, he said, "So I've been told, but nobody's ever offered proof."

"Next time, I'll pull out my phone and record you," came her impish reply. "I've been keeping an eye on dinner. It's smelling better all the time. I don't know how I resisted tasting it."

"Soon, soon," he told her. "Enjoying your book? Anything come up while I was asleep?"

"The storm is supposed to be changing over to ice, then rain. It'll be gone by morning. And Detective Samms called."

That name was like a punch in the gut. "He tracked you down, did he? What did he want?"

"Just as you said," Charlie told him. "He wanted to check out your alibi. I told him when you were at Rosie's, but he still wants a written statement. Next week is midterms so I told him he'd have to look me up at school, not at the club."

"I'm sure that made him happy, not that I really care much if Samms is happy or not."

"I know he's not happy. I tried to catch him out by asking what drugs they found at the scene. He didn't slip, but he did sound annoyed that I asked. Not that I care." She grinned.

Alex got up and headed into the kitchen to check on dinner. He had some expensive out-of-season asparagus in the fridge and decided to roast that with olive oil and garlic to go with the chicken. Charlie followed him into the kitchen and watched his every move as he prepped it.

"Can I help?" she asked again.

"Actually, yes. There's a cookie sheet in the drawer under the oven. Grab that please, and set the oven for 350."

Taking it from her, he arranged the asparagus on the sheet, added the oil and seasonings, and then started a pot of water boiling to cook the pasta. All the while, he was thinking about how to prove Spencer's involvement. Just as he was putting the asparagus in the oven and the pasta in the water, Charlie's phone rang again.

She looked at it and answered immediately. Once again, she started off with, "Hi, Alan." When he heard that name this time, Alex almost burned himself splashing boiling water from the pot.

"No, this is a good time," she said. "You told me you wouldn't call until tomorrow. What's up? You're shining me! Really? No, don't worry. It won't get out to the media. Thanks, Alan. Come by any time."

Alex couldn't wait. "What did he say?" he demanded in an impatient voice. "What showed up so quickly?"

"They found a white powder at the scene, on Walker's clothes and in his nose. It field-tested positive for meth. He's going to get me a detailed analysis when he can."

"That can't be right!" was Alex's angry retort. "Drugs, drugs, *drugs!* Every time I hear something about Walker's death, it comes back to drugs! Damn it. It makes no frigging sense!"

"Alex," Charlie said in as soothing a voice as she could muster, "calm down, and please tell me again why it's so impossible. Aren't there ways to cheat on drug tests?"

Shaking his head violently, Alex replied, "Maybe, maybe not. But they go after us three different ways, Charlie. Not only do we have to do the pee-in-a-cup routine, they take blood and hair as well."

Alex could see her putting on her scientist hat. "Hair? Hmm ... Traces do get deposited as the hair grows, so even if the it's been long enough for the substance to metabolize, it should still show up in the hair. That's a very high bar for a cheater to get over. Could it have been a first-time mistake?"

Again, the denial. "I don't buy it. Why do it at work? Why bring the stuff *into* the plant? The guards do random searches. Why do it at all when the next drug test is going to catch you and you'll wind up out on your ass? No, it's wrong." Then the light bulb went off. "There's only one thing that makes sense, and that's if the meth was used to kill him!"

Now it was Charlie's turn to disbelieve. "Now *that's* crazy," she said. "The person who killed him would have to have access *and* motive *and* means. Who could that be?"

"I can think of one person who has motive," he told her. Then he reiterated what he had told Jake and the two LEOs about the re-rack project and Frank Spencer. As he told her, he could see the doubt starting to show in her eyes.

"Okay, so he sounds like the kind of SOB who *would* do it and he has access. But is he big enough to take down Walker and hold him down while shooting meth up his nose? *Lots* of meth? I mean, where did he get the drugs? And what about the security system alibiing him?"

"That I don't know. Not yet anyway. I guess we have to wait for the autopsy results. If they show Walker was knocked out, or there's some other evidence that he was restrained, then the theory may work. Until then—"

The timer dinged for the pasta. Charlie declared, "Okay, that's it. No more death and dying tonight. You've made us a wonderful dinner that I can't wait to eat. You get the wine out and set the table while I take care of the rest. I found the strainer while you were asleep."

Alex opened his mouth to protest, closed it, and then gave Charlie a big hug. "Thank you. You're right. I can't tell you how glad I am you're here."

She held the hug for a few moments and then pushed him away. "Wine! Lots of wine! Move your ass."

"Yes, ma'am," he replied as he reached for the glasses.

CHAPTER 11

DINNER WAS A GREAT SUCCESS, AND Charlie's demand that Walker's death not be a topic of conversation was a big help. They ended up sharing a lot about themselves. Alex found out that it was Charlie's mother who was white and her father who was black. Also that she had a brother in the Marine Corps who had already served one tour in Iraq and was currently trying to make it into Force Recon. He also found out she'd spent two years traveling in Europe before starting college.

Charlie found out Alex had grown up around marines at Twenty-Nine Palms and that his was the first generation of the family not to do military service. Not by choice, but by getting marked 1Y—"unfit for induction or commission"—when he tried to go navy OCS after college.

The food was a big hit and so was the wine. Alex was happy he'd bought a couple of bottles of the Black Swan Pinot Grigio. They lingered over it for a long time before an awkward silence appeared.

Alex asked, "Interested in dessert? There's some strawberry ice cream in the freezer. Or coffee? My buddy Jake says I make the worst coffee in the world, but I've never had anybody else complain."

"No, thank you. It's been an awesome evening, but I think between the storm and the wine I'm about to crash. Do you mind?"

"Of course not," Alex replied. "Let's get you something to sleep in and you'll be all set."

He found her a T-shirt and added his robe, then grabbed a pillow, sheet, and blanket for himself. By the time he had the couch made up, Charlie was out of the bathroom, looking lost in Alex's robe, sleeves flopping. She tried to give him a hug, but the robe started to fall off, making them both laugh.

"Thank you for rescuing me, for a wonderful dinner, just…everything," she told him.

"My pleasure," Alex responded. "I never turn down a chance to rescue a damsel in distress, especially one as pretty as you."

"Good night, Alex," she said, standing up on her toes to give him a peck on the cheek. She was much shorter without her platforms.

"Good night," he told her. He stood aside so she could enter the bedroom through the kitchen and shut the completely symbolic door. After a trip to the bathroom, he went into the living room, wrapped himself in a blanket, and turned off the light. Thanks to the wine, it didn't take long before he fell asleep.

The next thing he knew, somebody was shaking him, telling him to wake up, and as he struggled up from the depths of sleep, he realized he was cold. He discovered he was squeezed up into the fetal position and his blanket felt like no protection at all.

"What?" he asked. "What's going on?"

"Alex, I think the power's out. The lights won't come on and it's really cold in here. Wake up!"

As he woke up, Alex realized the room was dark except for a glow in Charlie's hand, a flashlight app on her phone. No light came in from the streetlamps outside, the clock on the cable box was dark, and there was certainly a chill in the room.

Sitting up he exclaimed, "Great! That's just frigging great! Back in the old house, I had a generator for this sort of thing. Here, I've got nothing! Damn it to hell!"

Getting up, he wrapped the blanket around himself and peered out the windows. It soon became very obvious this house was the limit of the problem. Just fifty yards down the street, he could see streetlights and lights in houses. The other direction, up the hill, was dark.

"We must be at the end of the line, damn it," he told her. "From what I can see, the road looks clear, but maybe it's icy and somebody took out a pole."

Just then, his cell rang, and when he looked at the caller ID, it said,

"CT Alert System." He punched the answer button and then turned on the speakerphone so Charlie could hear. The mechanical voice started speaking. "This is the Connecticut Alert Emergency Notification System. This message is to inform you of power outages in the Jordan Cove and Rope Ferry Road areas of Waterford, Connecticut, plus parts of adjoining neighborhoods. Waterford DPW is already working on repairs. Residents are advised that many roads are still ice-covered and driving is extremely hazardous."

Alex hit the disconnect and made a noise of disgust. "If the roads are still too icy to drive, I don't know what to do. I can't take you home yet. Damn!"

Charlie turned the phone light so Alex could see her face. "I'll tell what we're going to do. I'm freezing in that bed and you're freezing out here. We're going to get your blanket and any others you have onto the bed and then we're going to snuggle up under them and keep each other warm."

Alex was glad Charlie couldn't see his face because his jaw dropped to his knees. It took two or three tries before he could get any sound to come out.

"Charlie, that's a bad idea in so many ways I don't know where to start."

"Too fucking bad, Sir Galahad. If you're really the gentleman you pretend to be, now's your chance to prove it. You didn't take me home and now I'm freezing my ass off in this shoebox. Get the goddamn blanket on the bed, get your ass in there, or I'm putting my clothes on and *walking* home, right now!"

Alex was stumped, outmaneuvered, completely flummoxed. Charlie turned the phone toward him and waited for his reply. Literally on the spot, Alex could not think of a single thing to say. After a few seconds, Charlie demanded, "Well? Last chance!"

With a big sigh of resignation, Alex told her, "Okay, I got you into this and I can't argue with your logic. Which side do I get?"

"That's more like it. For being such a good boy, you can have whatever side you usually sleep on."

"Thank you. That would be the kitchen side. Go around and help me get this blanket on the bed."

They both turned away. Alex grabbed his pillow then pulled the blanket from around himself and stuffed them both under one arm. He entered the bedroom from the kitchen door, stopping to retrieve a flashlight from a drawer next to the stove. He turned it on and placed it on top of the dresser so they could see enough to arrange the blanket.

Alex tossed a corner over to Charlie, who caught it, and together they quickly got it centered on the bed. He grabbed his robe from the foot of the bed where Charlie had put it and threw it on top. Alex turned off the flashlight and put it on the nightstand, then lifted the corner and crawled in. As he did so, he could feel the mattress move as Charlie crawled in on the other side but the room was too dark to see anything but a vague shape. He wiggled over toward the center of the bed until suddenly he and Charlie met up in the middle.

Forehead to forehead, he whispered to her, "Okay, how do you want to work this? Personally, I think it will be better if you turn over and let me snuggle up."

In the cold dark, she whispered back, "I think you're right." As she turned away from him, he slipped one arm under her pillow, the other around her waist, and pulled the two of them together. He gave her a quick kiss on the top of her head and whispered, "Good night, Charlie."

"Good night, Alex. See you in the morning."

He lay there, feeling the warmth of her slim body up against him, hardly daring to breathe. After what seemed a very long time, he felt her relax and her breathing go regular and deep. Then he finally closed his eyes to the black night and slipped into a different kind of darkness.

Somewhere in the back of his mind, Alex was getting annoyed. People were forever waking him up when all he wanted to do was sleep. "Go away!" he said to whoever was shaking his shoulder.

"I really wish I could, but I can't," a voice said. "Wake up, Alex!"

Memories flooded back in to Alex's waking mind. He opened his eyes and saw Charlie facing him from less than a foot distance, weak sunlight showing nothing but her face above the blanket.

"Good morning," he said to her.

"Good morning yourself. I was right before, and now I have proof. If you ever cause me trouble, I'll post the video I made of you snoring like a bear on YouTube."

"Hmmph," was his only reply. "Is the power still out? What time is it?"

"Yes, it is. But we have hot water. That was a nice surprise. And it's about seven. Can we please get up and get me back to the dorm? I have studying to do."

Alex pushed the blanket off and climbed over Charlie to look out the window at the street below. The sand and salt spread by the town during the night appeared to be having some effect. He turned back to Charlie and said. "Yeah, it looks like we might make it. Get dressed. We'll get some breakfast and then head out. I want to give it just a little more time. I promise you'll be home before nine."

"You first. It's cold out there! When I'm dressed, I want to leave, not wait around for you."

Alex reached for the clothes he'd left hanging over his desk chair the night before. He quickly shed his gym shorts then put on the freezing cold shirt and pants. Grabbing his shoes, he climbed over Charlie to get a clean pair of socks from his dresser. Shoes and socks on, he told her, "I'll brush my teeth while you're dressing. There's a little place right down the road called the Country Kitchen. From what I could see, they have power. We'll get breakfast there and be on our way."

"Only if I pick up the tab," Charlie responded. "I'm feeling a little too indebted to you."

"Whatever you want. Come on. Get going." As he headed for the bathroom, he could hear her starting to move.

"What if I don't want breakfast?" she shouted.

"You don't even know if Conn College has power!" he shouted back. "Let's take a bit of time to get warmed up, get some hot coffee into us, and give the roads a little more time to clear!"

Charlie made some reply he couldn't discern while his electric toothbrush was buzzing in his mouth. But by the time he'd finished, she was dressed and waiting at the bathroom door.

"My turn." They swapped places and Alex started to put on his boots. By the time he was finished lacing them up, she was done. He hit the remote starter on the key fob then unlocked the truck doors. He retrieved their coats from the closet then went to get Charlie's bag from the bedroom.

"Everything in here?" he asked her.

"Yes. Are you ready?"

"I'm ready if you are. Let me carry this. I'll go down first. Be very careful and hang on to the rail."

It turned out that Alex's landlord had already been busy. The landing and steps were almost clear and the descent was easy. The truck was another matter. It was encased in ice, and Alex couldn't even get his door open.

"To hell with this," he said as the engine hit the end of the ten-minute remote start run and stopped. "Let's let this run another ten and we'll walk over to eat." He restarted the engine with the remote. "Let me have your bag."

This obviously didn't make Charlie happy, but she could see the sense in it and handed him her bag. They skated down to the sidewalk and turned left toward the cafe. It was just on the other side of the church next to Alex's place, and even with the snow and ice, the walk only took a few minutes.

The cafe was, thankfully, both open and warm. They sat down at a table and ordered coffee as soon as the waitress appeared. By the time she was back, they had decided and placed their orders.

While waiting for the food, Alex broached the subject of the events of the previous day.

"Charlie, I'm really sorry you got trapped with me. I honestly thought that bringing you here was the best thing to do. I really feel I've made a mess of things between us and I apologize."

She looked at him over her coffee cup and said, "I don't know what I'm going to do with you. Yes, I wished I'd been able to make it back to the dorm, but I've got to say you lived up to your white knight standards. The storm wasn't your fault and you've been nothing but nice. I'm sorry I got mad at you last night when the power went out. If I have to be trapped in a blizzard with a guy, I guess you're the guy to be trapped with."

Alex gave out a sigh of relief and asked, "So we're good?"

"We are," Charlie said. "As long as the food is decent and you take me home right after we're done!"

"Deal. Here comes breakfast."

As they ate, the sun started to peek through the thinning clouds. By the time they were done, it was out in full force and having a good effect on the sidewalk and roads. When they made it back to the truck, the defroster, with a solar assist, had done its work. It only took a few minutes to clear off the truck enough to drive.

Once they were loaded up, Alex headed down through Waterford center toward New London. He decided to go up Colman Street since it was a main thoroughfare and more likely to be plowed. His judgment was sound.

There wasn't much talk during the drive. Mostly, they marveled at the ice-covered trees and power lines. Rather than fight the interchanges up by I-95, he turned right onto Broad, then left on Williams Street, which led him to the front of the campus. When he got close to the right turn into the campus loop, Charlie asked him to pull over.

"This is close enough," she told him. "You don't have to deliver me to my door. Actually, I'd rather you didn't."

"I understand. Well, we've survived a blizzard. Hopefully, there won't be any more for us to go through."

Charlie gave him a quick hug and said, "Thanks again. I'll call or e-mail you as soon as I hear anything from Alan."

There was Walker's death again. "I'll be waiting. Good luck on your exams."

And with that, she was out of the truck and heading for her dorm. Alex waited until she was out of sight, turned around, and headed for home. *So what am I going to do for the rest of the weekend? It's going to be a long three days!*

Chapter 12

THE REST OF THE WEEKEND DID indeed pass very slowly. The power came back on about ten in the morning, which was a huge relief. Alex spent a lot of time browsing Monster.com for jobs and tweaking his résumé. The rest of the time he spent watching old movies on TCM, reading, and thinking about Walker's death.

The one bright spot in the weekend was a call from Jake. His friend apologized for not calling earlier. Jake had lost both his power and landline, and cell phone service in his little hollow was nonexistent. He heated his home with wood so at least they didn't freeze.

Alex shared the information from the OCME's office he'd gotten through Charlie. Jake's response was, "Well, that fits with what the plant superintendent hinted at on Thursday. Until the autopsy is done, I don't think much more is going to happen. You still think Spencer had something to do with it, don't you?"

"Absolutely. I don't know how, but I'm sure he did. But you are right; it looks like waiting for the autopsy is all we can do right now."

Alex then went on to tell him about rescuing Charlie and the aftermath. He could hardly get the story out between Jake's laughter and comments. When he finished, Jake told him, "Only you, Alex. Only you could wind up in bed with a beautiful girl and do nothing but sleep. What a goddamn loser."

"Stuff it, Jake," was his friend's reply. "You know me better than that! She wasn't here because she wanted to be."

"I know. I know. I'm sorry. It's just so perfectly you."

Alex changed the subject to work schedules. "Will you be down this way next week? It looks like it's supposed to warm up a little bit. Want to try for an off-site lunch?"

"Sounds good to me. Let's see if things are a little more settled on Monday and go from there, okay?"

"Okay. Talk to you later, buddy." Their conversation ended and Alex was back alone with his thoughts. Inevitably, they turned to Walker's death.

We weren't even close. Why is his death getting to me so much? Come on, Alex, you know why. It's the injustice of it. Not only is he dead, it looks like the incident *is going to get swept under the rug. If he* was *murdered, and I think he was, that means his killer gets away with it and Walker's name is tarnished forever. I don't handle that kind of thing very well. I've always been the kind of person to stand up when I see something wrong, even when nobody else cares. "All it takes for evil to succeed is for a few good men to do nothing." I don't know how good a man I am, but I sure as hell can't sit back and do nothing!*

Chapter 13

Monday came as a relief. As far as going to work was concerned, it seemed like nothing had happened. Maybe, just maybe, the guards in the cage at the MAP were looking a little more closely at badges and taking a bit more time to match photos with faces, but that might have been all in his head.

The first reminder that things were not what they had been came when he got to his desk. His computer was on his desk when he got to it, but it was not hooked up. Evidently, the cops didn't think it was necessary to reconnect it. Alex wondered if the police were still holding onto any machines and if the returned ones were in operating condition. *Could be a busy morning,* he thought.

That did indeed turn out to be the case. Once he got his machine up and running, he discovered some waiting trouble tickets, and soon his phone started ringing with calls from users with all kinds of problems. While no machines were missing and nothing was actually broken, some computers had loose drive cables or power connectors. Some users had plugged network cables into the wrong port—that kind of garbage. It took him almost two hours to get everything under control before he could start looking at his reports.

As Alex downloaded the data from corporate, he suddenly realized he didn't know who he was going to give the reports to. *Who's going to fill Walker's job?*

Just as he was finishing up, he got an answer to that question. His phone rang and the caller ID showed Cynthia, Big Mike's admin assistant. Alex answered and Cynthia told him to come to Big Mike's office right away.

When Alex reached Mike's office, the door was open. Inside were three men. The first two were Big Mike and Detective Samms, WPD. The third was a short black man Alex remembered as a guy from Trippler HQ, but whose name he could not remember. *Great, time for another inquisition.*

Big Mike saw him in the doorway and gave a come-in gesture followed by pointing at the only remaining chair. Alex took it and waited.

"How're you holding up, Alex? How was your weekend?" asked Mike.

"Long and cold," was Alex's reply. He then turned his attention to the WPD man. "Your people were none too gentle with our equipment, Detective Samms. I had a lot of problems to deal with this morning."

Samms gave a tight little smile and replied, "I will pass your concerns on to the FBI, Mr. Strong. Their people did the forensic work on your computers, not us."

Alex gave a grunt in response and turned back to Big Mike. "What's up, Mike? What can I do for you?"

"Alex," he said, "this is Kevin Drummond from corporate. He and the detective want to ask you some questions about the re-rack project."

"Fine with me. Fire away."

Samms spoke first. "The FBI techs were able to recreate the report you gave to Mr. James. Can you tell us please why you thought it was sufficiently unusual that you needed to bring it to his attention?"

"Yes, I can. The burn rate, how fast the project is using up money, was not only high but accelerating. That is usually an indication of unexpected difficulties, something going wrong that is out of the defined project scope. The problem with this job is that, once we got the additional funds for the last big change, nothing coming in seemed to be out of scope but the burn rate kept going up."

Drummond spoke up. "What was that last big change? Was it the cast concrete wall?"

Alex nodded and said, "Yes, that was it. That mistake added a lot of cost and complexity to the job."

Back to Samms. "It's our understanding, Mr. Strong, that the error that led to that problem has been attributed to a Yankee Power employee?"

Alex nodded again. "Yes. Frank Spencer. He's the person who had the responsibility for the final approval of the project plans."

Drummond then asked him, "What would you think if we told you that Mr. Spencer is saying that specs were changed *after* he signed off on them? That he is, in fact, claiming that Walker James made the changes without his knowledge?"

Alex was dumbfounded. "You can't be serious. Why in the world would Walker do something like that?" *And blaming it on a dead man is a pretty contemptible thing to do!*

"His allegation," Drummond responded, "is that Mr. James had found a flaw in the accounting system that allowed him to divert the cost overruns into his own pocket." He held up his hand to silence Alex's protest. "Before you say anything, let me tell you that there is no evidence at this time to support that claim. Right, Detective?"

"That's correct. What we would like to know, Mr. Strong, is if you saw or heard anything that might corroborate his claim, or if you are aware of any mechanism by which funds might be diverted."

Alex shook his head violently. "No to both. The opposite is true. I saw Walker trying very hard to figure out what was going on and doing his best to correct it. As to moving money around, the answer is also no. I'm not an accountant. With Quicken's help, I can keep my own checking account balanced and that's about all."

The three men exchanged glances and their expressions seemed to indicate they were satisfied with Alex's answers. Then Samms spoke again.

"Mr. Strong, I know this isn't a pleasant question, but I must ask it. Do you have any knowledge, or even any suspicions, that Mr. James was involved in any way with illegal drugs?"

Even though he'd guessed this question was coming, it took all of Alex's willpower to keep himself under control. In the most even voice he could muster, he replied, "No, nothing. The substance-abuse checks we have to go through, both pre-employment and after we're hired, make that kind of thing virtually impossible to hide. I didn't socialize much with Walker, but I never saw him use drugs of any kind. To the best of my knowledge, he wasn't even a big drinker. May I ask why you're asking that question?"

Samms gave a miniscule shake of his head. "No, I'm sorry, Mr. Strong. I can't answer that at this time. This is still an open and ongoing investigation. I have no further questions for you. Your alibi checks out and, as you pointed out at our first meeting, the plant security system does not show you on the premises. Neither were there any recorded intrusion attempts around the time Mr. James died. Gentlemen?"

Big Mike spoke up. "Alex, you need to know that Kevin here is taking on Walker's duties until we can find a permanent replacement. I know I can count on you to fill him in on our daily process and help him out."

Alex turned his attention back to Kevin Drummond to give him a closer look. His inquiring look was met with a level gaze and a small smile. "Sure thing, Mike. Whatever it takes."

Drummond spoke up again. "It's been a few years since I've been at a field operation. I appreciate your willingness to help get me up to speed. When we're done here, I'll come and look you up."

Realizing his new supervisor had just dismissed him, Alex stood up to leave. "Today's reports are done. Come by whenever you're ready."

Big Mike stepped in, saying, "Thanks, Alex. See you later."

Alex exchanged good-byes with all three men and left. *Why do I get the feeling that that this Drummond guy and I are not going to get along?*

Since it was almost noon, Alex started gathering data from the project supervisors for his afternoon update. They were evidently pushing their crews hard, trying to make up work caused by the unexpected days off.

He'd been at it for about twenty minutes when Drummond came up to his desk. "Hello, Alex. Could you come into my office, please?"

Alex grabbed a notebook, pencil, and the morning reports and followed Drummond into what he still thought of as Walker's office. But there was very little reminiscent of his dead boss. Between the crime scene techs and Drummond, the place had been cleaned out. Alex had to fight down the feelings caused by knowing this was the last place he'd seen Walker alive and the place where he'd died.

Drummond obviously had no such compunctions. He quickly sat down in Walker's old chair, pointedly not asking Alex to sit.

"I've looked over reports for the last month," he began. "Everything except the re-rack building appears to be in good order. The client has suspended work on that until they have done some additional digging into the financial aspects Detective Samms spoke about." He paused, as if to let Alex ask questions, but he had none.

"That being the case, I think we can keep the current roster of reports. Is it possible for you to come in an hour earlier so we can be sure to have them for the client by noon?"

Alex responded, "Yes, I can, but that won't help better the odds that the report will be done on time."

"And why is that?" asked Drummond.

"The single most frequent delay in getting the morning report done is failure of the batch job from corporate that gives me the roll-up figures. If that fails, there's no way to get another one until somebody from IT at headquarters gets in, sees the trouble ticket, and reruns the job. On top of that, I frequently need data from the project supervisors, and tracking them down takes time."

Instantly, Alex knew he had hit a sore point. *What did I say?*

Looking offended, Drummond told him, "I believe you're speaking about the consolidated man-hour and cost-summary report. I'm the person who designed that report. I'm surprised to hear that you have problems with it."

Oh crap. I just put my foot in that one. Aloud, he continued. "There's nothing wrong with the report. It gives us exactly the data we need. It's something in the batch process that's failing. Both Walker and I have contacted IT about the issue numerous times, but there never seems to be any progress."

Looking somewhat mollified, Drummond replied, "Very well. I'll contact the IT manager myself and ask about the problem. If it continues to be an issue, please let me know."

"Certainly. Anything else?"

"I know that your supervisor's untimely death must have been difficult for you. However, we need to get the work back on track. I understand from Detective Samms that you had some … *speculations* concerning Mr. James' death. I want to make sure you understand that we need to leave the police free to do their job without *interference*."

For the second time that day, Alex was stunned. *He's telling me not to make waves, or else. He doesn't give a damn about Walker being murdered. He just doesn't want to rock the boat with YP!*

"I understand perfectly," he told Drummond.

"Fine, fine. I'm sure we'll work well together. Are those the morning reports you have? Fine. Just leave them with me. I'll go over them and get back to you with any questions. Let's schedule the update meeting for three thirty, shall we?"

Pompous ass, thought Alex. "See you at three thirty, sir."

"No need for the 'sir.' Kevin is fine."

"Okay, Kevin. Three thirty."

"Thank you, Alex. That will be all for now." He turned his face to his desk in dismissal.

Double pompous ass, Alex thought as he turned to leave.

Alex had just reached his desk when his cell phone started to vibrate. He kept it on that setting at work because of the noise level in the bullpen next door. When he looked at the caller ID, he saw it was blocked. *I bet that's Charlie. She doesn't realize that I know her number now. Somehow, I don't think it's the right time to tell her.* He gave a quick smile and hit the connect button. "Hi, honey, ready for midterms?"

It was Charlie, but she started with "How did you know it was me? I blocked my number."

"I don't get that many blocked calls, sweetheart. Just a good guess."

"Okay, I'll buy that. Anyway, my first exam is done and it went well. But that's not why I called. I got a call from Alan this morning, a voice mail actually; he called when I was in class. He's going to e-mail me the exact chemical signature of the meth they found in Walker. He also wanted me to know they're almost done with the autopsy and he'll get me a report as soon as he can. How are you doing?"

His desk was too public a spot to really answer that question. "I have a new boss, and I had another chat with Samms this morning. I'll send you an e-mail with the details."

"Can't talk? Okay, I get it. Take care, sweetie."

"You too," Alex told her. "Good luck on the rest of your exams."

After killing the call, Alex sat down and wrote a quick e-mail summarizing the meeting with Big Mike, Samms, and Drummond. He sent that off to Charlie then started looking through his work e-mail for new trouble tickets. Finding a few, he set off to deal with them before lunch.

I wonder how the chemical composition of the meth can help us. Right now we have nothing to match it to. Where did it come from?

CHAPTER 14

THE THREE THIRTY MEETING WITH DRUMMOND was more of the same. The man's questions, especially about the re-rack building, were obviously intended to uncover if Walker had been involved in siphoning money from the project. After a while, it got to the point where the probing questions began to poke into possible involvement on Alex's part. That was too much.

"Look, Kevin, by now, the cops have checked my bank accounts and credit cards. I know they didn't find anything because there's nothing to find. I got divorced recently and we split the money down the middle. My credit card balance gets paid off every month, and the only installment debt I have is my truck. I'm sure corporate would love to be able to hand the customer somebody's head on a platter for this job, but it's not me. I don't think it was Walker either. I understand it won't make any points with the client if we discover it was one of their people stealing their money, but I still think Frank—"

Drummond held up his hand to stop him there. "I know your feelings about Mr. Spencer. I imagine the police are looking at his financial history as well. However, he doesn't work for Trippler and you do. I can't do anything about him, but I do have instructions from corporate to try and find out if any Trippler employee is guilty of fraud. My apologies if my questions make you uncomfortable, but I believe they are necessary."

Alex responded, "Then I wish you'd just ask instead of fishing around." He changed the direction of the conversation by standing up and saying, "If you don't have any further questions about the current projects, I'd like to check for any last-minute trouble tickets and brass out. My shift is over at five."

Drummond was not pleased, but unscheduled OT for a Trippler employee wasn't going to make the customer happy and that counted for more. "Very well. I will send you an e-mail if I have any more questions. Thank you."

Alex left Drummond's office, fuming at the treatment he'd received. He got to his desk, saw that nothing new had come in, and shut down his machine.

Still fuming, he got into his coat and left the building. After he brassed out, he pulled out his cell phone and punched the speed-dial number for Jake as he quick-marched to the MAP.

"Hey, Alex, what's up? How'd the first day back go?" his friend asked.

"Crummy. I have a new boss who is hell-bent on hanging either Walker or me for the re-rack fiasco." Then he related the discussions he'd had with Drummond.

Jake's response was completely unexpected. "I'm sorry to tell you this, but it's probably going to get worse. We had a visitor from the Environmental Protection Agency today. He came to look at the plans for the new cooling water outlets for Unit II. But the story going around is that he saw the re-rack building and asked what it was. After the guy showing him around told him, the EPA engineer asked to see the environmental master plan map for the site. Once he got a look at it, he told our guy that the building is sitting on a wetlands area and we'd never gotten a permit from EPA to build there. Bottom line, not only are we facing a huge fine but the building has to come down, like yesterday, and be moved to a new location. What do you think about that?"

Alex was so astonished by what he heard that he stopped in his tracks. Profanity was too weak to express his shock. "You have *got* to be kidding me! How in the world did something like that slip through the cracks? Who ..."

Even as he framed the question, the answer came to him. "Spencer. He was the project manager. He had to sign off on all aspects of the project. Just like the height spec error, he let this one get by him too. Is he really that goddamn incompetent?"

"He hasn't been up to now," Jake told him. "Stop and think about it a little and see if you come up with the same thought I did."

Alex resumed his rapid pace toward the exit, thinking furiously about what his friend had just told him. The answer burst upon him just as he reached the MAP and he stopped dead again to tell Jake his answer. "Every 'mistake' the SOB made resulted in the costs going up, *way* up. By the time the tear-down and move is complete, the project will cost eight or ten times more than the original estimate! There *must* be some way he's channeling the excess funds to himself. Why can't the cops find it?"

"I don't know," was his friend's grim reply. "All I can tell you is that my management is incredibly pissed off. Spencer may well lose his job over this."

"Maybe that's what he wants," said Alex. "Maybe he figures he's milked the scam for everything it's worth and it's time to bail. But why now?"

Another bombshell exploded in Alex's brain as he went through the turnstile and dropped his badge at the desk. *Sparkle! Walker was onto his scheme so Spencer killed him. Now the old sod thinks it's time for him and his girlfriend to take his ill-gotten gains and settle down in Rio!*

"Jake, did you know that Spencer is involved with one of the dancers at Rosie's? A girl named Sparkle?" The silence from the other end was enough of an answer. "What if this whole scam is to get enough money for them to run away together? Charlie told me their relationship was more 'commercial' than ours is. Could all this be about Spencer having a midlife crisis?"

"Alex, I don't know. It makes some kind of perverted sense, but most guys go out and buy a sports car. I still can't see how the money ends up in Spencer's pocket."

"Me neither," his friend replied. "But it does give us another theory to work on. Let's give it some time to percolate and we'll compare notes. How about lunch tomorrow? Off-site? I could stand to score some points with my new boss. It won't hurt for him to know I have a personal relationship with a senior YP engineer."

"Yeah, tomorrow should work," Jake replied. "I'll meet you at your office. I'll show up a little early and, if you happen to be meeting with your new boss, I'll 'ask' him if I can take you away for an hour or so. How's that sound?"

"Perfect, Jake. Just perfect. I'll see you tomorrow."

"You got it. Bye now." He killed the call.

Alex found his truck in the sea of vehicles in the MAP parking lot and headed home. Even though his eyes were on the road, his mind was someplace else. He was thinking hard about how the money could get moved from YP to Spencer and not coming up with any answers.

Dinner tonight was soup, a staple of Alex's during the cold seasons of the year. He'd make up a pot over the weekend and eat it up during the week. Today, he bypassed the apartment and stopped at a Dunkin' Donuts near the town center to pick up a couple of croissants to go with the corn chowder.

It wasn't quite dark when he made it home. *Spring is just over a month away. I can tell the days are getting longer. No more of that getting up in the dark and going home in the dark. I swear that rots my brain ...*

Since it was still a bit early, Alex put the soup on the stove, letting it heat slowly instead of zapping it in the microwave. He sat down at his computer and checked his mail and some of his regular sites. He went back to the Web forum where he'd found so much information about WATCHDOG to see if there were any new threads or posts since his first visit. There wasn't much. As a topic, WATCHDOG seemed to have played out for the moment.

He was just about to check the soup when he got a new mail announcement. His personal choice was a bugle playing "mail call". The return address was charliethedancer@gmail.com, and the message had an attachment!

Hot damn, he thought. *This must be the ME's report.* He started to open the message but remembered the soup on the stove. *Almost burned dinner. Can't have that!*

In a couple of minutes, he returned with a cup of soup and a croissant. He opened up the message, and it turned out to be a one-liner: "ME report attached. E-mail when you've read it."

Alex had seen only one autopsy report in his life before now. Compared to this one, the other was a comic book. The report he was looking at contained the ME's narration, full toxicology screen, and photographs of significant findings. The pictures were something he hadn't expected, and he quickly lost interest in dinner.

The tox screen and the final determination of cause of death soon drew his attention. "Cardiovascular collapse as a consequence of methamphetamine overdose." Time of death was between 9:00 PM and midnight. *It* was *meth that killed Walker! But where did it come from? Why did he take it?*

One thing he quickly discovered was that the toxicology findings came from blood drawn from the chest cavity. *They didn't test his hair! That would have shown whether or not he had a history of drug abuse. Damn it. I can buy a kit at the corner drugstore to do that!*

The rest of the report was best summed up by the term *unremarkable.* The same term appeared many times in the report. When he finished, Alex sent an e-mail to Charlie that he was done reading.

By the time he'd finished his croissant and gotten the crumbs out of the keyboard, his phone was ringing. He smiled at the blocked number and answered it. "Hi, honey. How's it going?"

He could hear fatigue in Charlie's voice as she answered. "Hi, Alex. My second exam was long and tough. I've got two more tomorrow then I'm done. I need to study, but I wanted to talk about the report Alan sent me. Let me ask you what you think first."

Alex thought a moment and then told her, "Well, I wish they'd done a drug screen on his hair to show if he had a history of abuse. That's the main thing. The other thing is, well, how little there is. Nothing but the drug-related heart attack. Can you call it that?"

Charlie replied, "It's as good a term as any. But did you see the concentration of meth in his blood?"

Alex paged down to the tox screen and found the number: 140mg/kg. He quoted it to her and asked, "Is that high?"

"High? It's through the freaking roof! The LD50 point (where 50 percent die) in rats is like 9mg/kg. They don't do LD50 testing on humans for illegal drugs, but this is a lethal level. I can't imagine how anybody could get that much meth into themselves voluntarily. That's a red flag for me.

"The next thing is what you picked up on. There's no bruising or other injuries. A person who overdoses on meth starts to run a fever. They can have convulsions. If he was thrashing around in his office, you'd think he'd hit something, cut or bruised his hands or arms. That's the second red flag."

Alex considered her words for a few moments then asked, "Charlie, do you have any ideas about what all that means?"

Charlie also took her time in replying. "When it comes to the amount, it seems to me it must have been forced into him somehow. The autopsy says that meth was found in his nose, sinuses, trachea, and lungs, so he inhaled it. It also says there was some minor damage to the lungs but not enough to be significant. Well, it just could be that the meth was forced into him, maybe even blown in. That would explain a lot."

Alex's mind was racing, combining Charlie's information along with the his talks with Drummond and Detective Samms. Just as he had earlier with Jake, Alex gave a synopsis of his meetings. Then he filled her in on what Jake had told him about the re-rack building and Spencer likely getting the boot. Lastly, he told her about his theory that Spencer and his girlfriend might be getting ready to run off together.

"Charlie, I need you to do me a favor. You said your last exams are tomorrow. Will you be back at the club tomorrow night?"

"I expect so, Alex. I'll get a nap in the afternoon and then go in. Why?"

"I want you to keep an eye on Sparkle. She probably won't talk to you because she knows about me. Try talking to the other ladies. Maybe they know if Sparkle has any plans to take time off, or if she's making noises about quitting. Can you do that for me, please?"

"I suppose so," she drawled. "I don't feel right about it. There's still no evidence her sugar daddy was at the plant that night, is there?"

"No," Alex admitted, "there isn't. That's still a missing piece of the puzzle, and it's a big piece, but to fill it in, we need more data. Please?"

"Well, I do agree with you that there seems to be something fishy about Sparkle and her Frankie. Let me think it over." Then her voice took on a roguish tone. "What's in it for me, Alex?"

Alex had to shift gears and think fast. "How about an airplane ride? I've got a ton of time off on the books. Let's take an afternoon and go fly. How's that sound?"

"That sounds so cool. Okay, you've got a deal. For that, I'll even call my friend at the FBI field office and see what she says. So far, she hasn't been any help, but that could change. Want me to call you on Wednesday?"

"That or e-mail," Alex told her. "Whatever is easier."

"Will do. Look, I've got to get back to studying. My first test tomorrow is at eight."

"Go to it, Charlie. Good luck. Talk to you soon. Good night, sweetheart."

"Good night, Alex. Later."

So we still don't know where the drugs came from and how Spencer got into the plant without WATCHDOG knowing about it. That's assuming he did get in. Maybe Drummond is right, Alex. Maybe you're blind to any other possibilities because Spencer is such a pain in the ass. But there's still the financial connection. I'll bet my last dollar that somebody from YP is siphoning off money, and who fits better than Spencer?

Alex wandered back into the kitchen and poured out a second cup of soup. By now, it was cold, so he zapped the soup for a minute and followed it with a buttered croissant. In three minutes, he was plopped down in the only living room chair, scrolling through the channel guide for something to watch. As he scrolled past the PBS channel, he caught sight of an episode of *Sherlock Holmes*, "The Empty House," starring Jeremy Brett. *Fitting,* Alex thought. *It's a locked-room mystery. Pity I can't solve this one as easily as Holmes does! What the hell. It will kill some time.* He flipped to WGBH and watched until he couldn't keep his eyes open any longer.

CHAPTER 15

THE NEXT MORNING, ALEX WAS VERY careful to delay the morning report until almost lunchtime. It really wasn't hard to do. He just had to request confirmation on the change orders for the re-rack building and wait until it came in from all the involved parties. That was normal procedure. It was just fortuitous that those change orders came in on the morning he wanted to throw a wrench into the works.

Five minutes into his meeting with Kevin Drummond, Alex heard a knock on the door behind him. When he looked over his shoulder, there was Jake, as promised.

Drummond looked annoyed at the interruption, and then he noticed the imposing person standing outside his door was wearing a white hardhat with a gold band around it. This marked him as a senior staffer with Yankee Power and therefore somebody to be polite to.

"May I help you?" he inquired.

"I sure hope so," Jake replied. "My name is Jake Campbell. I'm one of the supervising project mangers here. I heard you were coming onboard as Walker James' replacement and I wanted to introduce myself. I also wondered if I could steal away my buddy Alex here for an off-site lunch. We're very old friends and haven't seen much of each other lately. We've got a lot of catching up to do."

As he spoke, Jake moved up against Drummond's desk where he towered above the smaller man. Jake put out his hand and, even after he stood up to shake it, Drummond was still dwarfed by Alex's friend.

Good job, Jake. Intimidate him physically at the same time you establish the pecking order. Nice!

Drummond introduced himself but then seemed at a loss about what to say next. Finally, he said, "We were just getting started on our status update meeting. It shouldn't take long. Perhaps ten or fifteen minutes?"

Jake shook his leonine head. "Sorry, I've got to head up to HQ for a one-thirty meeting with the senior VP for nuclear power. Tell you what. Why can't Alex leave the reports with you to look over during lunch and you can ask him any questions you have when he gets back. How's that sound?"

Game, set, match to the big guy from the client! Get me off-site for lunch while making Drummond work through. Sweet!

Drummond gaped at Jake for a few seconds then closed his mouth and opened it again to speak. "Well, I guess that would be all right, Mr. Campbell, is it?" Then he turned to Alex and said, "Alex, I'll see you after lunch. Please check with me when you get back."

"Sure thing, Kevin," Alex responded. "Jake, good to see you. Just let me grab my coat and we'll head out."

In a couple of minutes, the two friends were out of Trippler's offices. After Alex brassed out, they headed for the ALTERNATE ACCESS POINT. The AAP was on the opposite side of the site from the MAP and Trippler's trailers. Since there was insufficient parking outside the AAP to handle all the contractor's employees, the AAP was used almost exclusively by Yankee Power personnel and visitors.

Once they were out of sight of his office, Alex grabbed Jake in a bear hug and pounded him on his back. "You bastard! That was absolutely magnificent! You took him down more pegs than a cribbage board!"

Jake returned the hug and laughed out loud. "I was pretty good, wasn't I? I rehearsed that all damn morning."

"You deserve an Oscar for that performance, let me tell you!"

"Thank you. So where to for lunch?" Jake asked. "The Sunset?"

"Works for me. You really got a meeting in Hartford?"

"Yeah, but not until later. We won't have to rush," Jake replied.

By this time, they had arrived at the AAP and surrendered their badges. Being an "early in" person, Jake's car was parked near the exit.

They climbed into the well-worn Jetta and drove off, still bantering about Jake's performance.

They got to Sunset Ribs, were shown to a table, and ordered quickly. Alex knew if he went for the big platter of ribs, he'd fight to stay awake all afternoon. Instead, he ordered a brisket sandwich while Jake ordered the pulled pork. Once their drinks arrived, Alex got serious.

"I got an e-mail from Charlie last night. It had the medical examiner's report attached. After I read it, she called me and we talked about the results."

"And what did it say?" his friend asked.

"First thing, it confirmed the rumors going around. The cause of death was a methamphetamine overdose that resulted in heart failure. But there were a couple things that really bugged Charlie. One was the level of meth in his blood. It was huge, way more than anybody would take to get high."

"That sounds suspicious right there," Jake interrupted.

"Right. The second thing was a lack of any bruising or other injuries. She thinks he would have gone into convulsions and should be more banged up from hitting things. The drug was inhaled and there was some slight damage to his lungs. It could be from the drug, but just possibly somebody forcibly squirted the stuff up his nose. That's Charlie's opinion. There's nothing in the ME's report about that."

"What about the girlfriend?" Jake asked.

"Charlie's done with midterms today and going back to work tonight. She's going to keep an eye on Sparkle for me and ask the other dancers about the Spencer/Sparkle connection."

Jake's eyebrows went up at that. "How much did that cost you? It sure as hell can't be your good looks!"

Alex smiled and told him, "I got off easy. I promised her a ride in the Cardinal. She thinks it's really cool that I'm a pilot and own an airplane."

"That's the way it is with airplanes," Jake said. "They either attract or repel 100 percent, no in-between. Didn't you tell me once that when you were in college you always asked a girl out flying for the first date? And if she said no, that was it, right then and there?"

Alex laughed and confirmed Jake's recollection. Then he turned back to serious matters. "What are you hearing on the YP side about the investigation? Anything at all?"

"Lots of digging into work records and financial files. The FBI has been around a lot. They're trying to find how funds could have been siphoned off, but nothing is showing up. But I've got worse news for you. Since Walker is dead, my management is going up the ladder to find somebody responsible for the re-rack fiasco. I think Big Mike might be out the door."

This revelation rocked Alex to his core, and it came just as the food arrived. He used the enforced silence caused by the presence of the waitress to sort out his thoughts and feelings.

Once she left he told Jake, "That is just plain wrong. The approval chain belongs to YP. We only do a review if we're specifically tasked to do so. What a crock!"

Jake nodded his head in agreement as he took a big bite of his sandwich. He pouched the bite in one cheek and mumbled, "I'm with you; it sucks. But they've got the gold so they make the rules." He chewed, swallowed, and continued. "The fact that drugs were involved in Walker's death won't help either. They'll use that to make a case for incompetent management. Hell, if they do that, you guys will probably lose your contract."

The prospect of unemployment didn't help Alex's nerves. Lunch didn't look very appetizing all of a sudden. Jake picked up on that right away.

"Relax. If Trippler goes down the toilet, I can probably find you a spot in my group. Don't sweat it. Eat."

With that reassurance, Alex returned to his meal. They ate in silence for a while and then Jake asked the $64,000 question. "Any luck figuring out how Spencer could have gotten into the plant to kill Walker? Honestly, that's the biggest hole you still have in your theory."

Switching to his coleslaw, Alex chewed and thought before answering. "No, not really. Getting through the fence unnoticed is impossible, as far as I know. Did I ever tell you about the pigeons?"

The sudden change in subject took Jake off guard. "Pigeons? What pigeons? What the hell are you talking about?"

"One day I got curious about how sensitive the motion detectors between the two fences really are. So I stopped at a hardware store a few months ago and picked up some birdseed."

"Uh, oh. I can see where this is going," Jake interjected.

Alex gave a sage nod. "I went walking along the inner fence, throwing birdseed into the gap. The birdseed wasn't enough to set off the alarms and I always had my back to the nearest camera when I tossed it in. After I'd seeded about one hundred feet of fence line, I broke off and headed to the Roach Coach. After about five minutes, pigeons started showing up. One, two, four, ten, twenty; a whole damn flock of them. No outside alarms went off, but a couple of guards came running out to that section of fence, going hell-for-leather. They gave it a good going over to make sure nothing had been cut, but all they found was a bunch of pigeons pecking at the ground. Not much they could do about that, was there?"

For a moment, Alex thought Jake was going to have a stroke. He laughed so hard he got beet red. When he finally stopped laughing, it took another minute for him to stop crying.

"That is funniest story I have heard in ages! I don't care if it's true or not, it should be!"

"It is," said Alex. "So vehicle gates are controlled by the guard force, and people go in and out through the access points. It still makes no sense, does it?"

"Nope. But you, old buddy, have got to stop obsessing about this. If you don't, you're going to get your ass in a sling at work and I won't be able to rescue you, not if you get fired for cause."

While he appreciated his friend's concern, Alex didn't feel the same way about the rebuke. "Let me worry about that. I was looking when I found this job. I'll find another if I need it."

Jake gave a shrug then continued. "Whatever you say. Hey, it's starting to get late. We don't want to use up all the cred I generated for you this morning in one shot. Time to go."

Alex reached for his wallet but Jake motioned him to put it away. "This one's on me. You can get the next one." Jake looked at the check and dropped money on top of it.

"Fair enough." They both stood up and headed for the door.

The ride back to the Point was a quiet one. Jake drove right up to the

AAP to drop Alex off. They sat there for a moment, and then Jake spoke one more time. "Alex, be careful. If somebody *did* kill Walker, he's still out there. You go poking around too much and you might be next on the list."

Alex started at these words. The possibility had never really occurred to him before. "That's a good point. I'll have to keep that in mind, won't I?" *Yes, I'll keep it in mind. If I push hard enough, maybe I can flush out the bastard!*

The two friends gave each other a long look, and then Alex got out of the car. He reached back in to shake Jake's hand. "See you, brother." Then he closed the door, watched his friend drive away, and waved as he made the left toward the access road. He stood there for a few moments, thinking about his friend's warning, then turned and went into the AAP to retrieve his badge. *It's time to go face Drummond. What a way to make a living!*

As soon as he got back to Trippler's office trailer, Alex peeled off his coat and headed for Drummond's office. The door was open, so he knocked on the doorframe. Drummond was looking down, studying a sheaf of plans on his desk. Alex was hit with a major case of *déjà vu*. The plans Drummond was studying were for the re-rack building! Alex was immediately reminded about the time he walked in on Walker studying the same plans.

Just as Walker had done, Drummond looked up from the drawings then motioned him in and gestured for him to sit.

"Have a nice lunch?" he asked. "If I may ask, just what is your relationship with Mr. Campbell?"

Alex ignored the lunch dig and took a seat before replying. "We've known each other since junior high. I was best man at his first wedding. I introduced him to his second wife. We've been best friends for over twenty years."

"I see" was Drummond's only reply. He studied Alex's face for a few moments and then shifted gears to business. "What can you tell me about this re-rack building project?" He gestured at the plans.

"The whole thing has been a mess from day one. The latest snafu, finding out that the client didn't have a permit to build on the wetlands area, is just icing on the cake. Has YP decided if they are actually going to have us move the building?"

"My understanding is that has yet to be decided. All of our work orders so far are for estimates and to define the scope of work. It is also my understanding that a new project manager will be assigned from Yankee Power."

Alex knew better than to gloat in front of Drummond. "So Frank Spencer is getting pulled off the job? Is he being reassigned to something else or will he be leaving YP?"

Drummond gave a sniff and then said, "That is not our concern, Alex. Our concern is to keep this project, all our projects for that matter, on schedule and on budget. Your reports are an important tool in making sure that happens. I trust that there won't be too many days like today?"

Alex stared Drummond straight in the eyes for a full five seconds before replying. "I doubt it. Whatever happens, you can rest assured that my reports will be up to date and the systems on-site will be kept up and running. That's my job."

"Fine, fine" was Drummond's reply, though his tone said anything but. "Shall we start going over these current projects and the estimates for the re-rack move?"

That's what they did for the next two hours. Time and again during those one hundred and twenty minutes, the thought that kept running through Alex's mind was *What a way to make a living!* Then suddenly it came to him. *Maybe it's a good way to get somebody to try and kill you, too.*

CHAPTER 16

WHILE ALEX WAS SUFFERING THROUGH HIS marathon session with Drummond, Charlie was getting ready for her shift at Rosie's. As she packed up her outfits for the night, her mind was a jumble of conflicting thoughts and feelings. *I can't believe it! I am part of an honest to God murder investigation. How the hell did I let myself get involved in this? I mean he's kind of good-looking, and he is sweet, but it was his friend that died, not mine. Why am I helping him?*

The more she thought about it, the more Charlie realized there was more at work than whatever feelings she may have developed for Alex. *I've spent almost four years learning how to do this. I've spent years reading books, going to lectures, spent hundreds of hours in labs, spent weeks doing internships, all to learn how to gather evidence and solve crimes.* This *is what I've wanted to do since I was a little girl. I'm doing it because it's what I want to do.*

With her mind made up, for the moment at least, Charlie headed downstairs and got into the rental car she was driving while hers was still in the shop getting the front end straightened out. Thankfully, she was still on her parents' policy so the rental was covered. Otherwise, getting to work would be a big problem.

While she drove, Charlie started thinking about who to approach at the club and how. *Diamond's my best friend, but is she the most connected?* Then she remembered something Alex had said to her three or four days earlier. He'd asked her if he was a major topic of discussion among the other girls. *I told him about Diamond, and then he said ... What did he say? "Now I have the best friend and the den mother identified." He was talking about Tanya! Damn, he's right. Tanya is the den mother of the place. She's the one who keeps an eye on* all *of us!*

By the time she reached Rosie's, Charlie's resolve to talk to Tanya about Sparkle and Frank Spencer had stiffened. She still wasn't 100 percent sure it was the right thing to do, but she was sure that Tanya was the one to go to.

Charlie was a little early. Her subconscious eagerness to talk to Tanya evidently translated to a slightly heavier foot on the accelerator. She came in through the front entrance then stood at the door and looked over the main floor. Tanya was nowhere to be seen. Nor, she noticed, was Sparkle. She checked in with Bill, the manager, and then went downstairs to get changed.

The dressing room was anything but glamorous. The cinder-block walls were painted a sick green. Department store-style clothing racks were pushed up against them for the dancers' street clothes and costumes.

The lighting consisted of a couple of overhead fluorescent fixtures with half the tubes removed. The main illumination came from lights surrounding the large mirror on one wall, and half a dozen cheap plastic chairs were pulled up to a countertop in front of the mirror. Used tissues and cotton wipes were scattered on the counter and floor—the small wastebaskets in the room were overflowing with them.

Charlie hung her coat on one of the racks then pulled her top off over her head. Anything that could mess up the makeup job had to go first. She pulled a short robe out of her bag and put it on. It wasn't much, but it helped keep her warm while working on her face. She didn't need a concealer yet, so her first move was to apply a new Sephora blush she'd found called Make Up Forever in a plum tone.

Her eyes took a lot of care to get just right. First, she used a puffy brush to lay down a base for her eye shadow, IMAN Tiger Eye, followed by a Chanel liner. The lower lash line was an Amazonian clay liner—waterproof because she could certainly work up a sweat when dancing. The final touch on her eyes was a Sephora waterproof mascara. She was lucky to have great natural lashes and not need much help.

Her lips came last. Charlie used a Mac Cosmetics liner first, then NARS Jungle Red lipstick. This was too matte by itself, so she added an

IMAN lip shine on top of it. She gave herself a close inspection, flashed a practice smile at the mirror, and decided she was ready to see and be seen.

She quickly skinned out of the rest of her clothes then pulled a jar of coco butter moisturizer from her bag and applied it everywhere she could reach, rubbing it in well and using a small towel to get the excess. This was a regular ritual, three or four times a day.

By now, she was starting to shiver, so Charlie quickly picked out her first costume for the night: a very short, black, wrap-around dress with a red G-string underneath. After slipping on red six-inch platforms, Charlie grabbed the little purse where she kept her essentials and headed upstairs. It was always warmer up there.

As she always did, Charlie paused at the entrance to the main room to survey the people there. She was surprised to see Tanya, already in costume, sitting at one of the tall tables near the bar. *She must have been outside grabbing a smoke when I came in. How did I miss her bag downstairs?*

Taking a deep breath, she walked over to greet her friend. After a quick hug and a kiss, Charlie sat down. Alanna was there in a second to take her order, but Charlie just asked for a glass of water. Right now, she needed a clear head.

They talked about Charlie's exams, the storm, and some other idle chitchat. Then Tanya gave Charlie a good hard look and said, "Sweetie, there's something on your mind. Is it problems with Alex?"

Charlie gave a wan smile and responded, "No. Well, sort of. You know his boss died, right? Well, it's beginning to look like he was helped along. Alex really thinks that Frank Spencer, the guy Sparkle hangs with, has something to do with it."

To Charlie's surprise, Tanya didn't burst out laughing or even smile. She stared at Charlie for a few seconds before she responded. "I never liked that guy much, Charlie. He throws way too much money around. Sparkle is too much of a party girl to resist that kind of temptation, know what I mean?"

"Party girl?" Charlie responded. "I've never seen her do anything more than pink lemonade shooters."

Tanya gave her a wry look and said, "She doesn't around here, at least not in the open. She's smarter than that. But there are times when she's come into work a little wild. It's hard to tell with someone like her, you know?"

With this insight, Charlie's mind went into overdrive trying to remember any incidents that went along with what Tanya was telling her. Looking back, she remembered times when she walked into the dressing room or the restroom and saw Sparkle give a start, look a little guilty, and avoid eye contact with her. *Damn*, she thought, *she just might be using. But what?*

Wait a minute! Spencer came in here and talked to her the night Alex's boss died. I think she left early that night too. Said she wasn't feeling well. Could she have something to do with the murder?

Evidently, Charlie's thoughts were playing out on her face, because Tanya asked her, "What are you thinking, sweetie?"

It took a couple of tries for Charlie to get the words out. "Frank Spencer showed up the night Alex's boss was killed." In her mind, she had crossed a threshold: this was a murder. "She took off early that night, not long after he got here. God, what time was that?"

Tanya raised her arm and waved to Bill, the burly club manager. When he arrived at the table, she asked him what time Sparkle had gone home sick.

Bill wasn't the curious sort, and maybe not too bright, but he knew the dancers' schedules to the minute and remembered everything that happened in the club.

"She left just after eight, complained she felt sick. Didn't look sick to me, but what am I going to do, take her temperature?" Tanya thanked him and he wandered back to the door, stopping to give Alanna's ass a quick squeeze.

"Does that mean anything to you, sweetie?" asked Tanya.

Charlie nodded and put her lips close to Tanya's so that it was certain nobody could hear what she said to Tanya. "Alex's boss was killed between nine and midnight. Did she leave with Frank?"

After Charlie pulled back, Tanya shook her head no. Charlie leaned forward again to ask, "Do you have any idea what she uses?" Again, a shake of Tanya's head in reply.

I guess it could be meth, Charlie thought. *I can lay hands on a field test kit, easy. But that won't tell me enough. If I can get a sample, I could run it through the mass spectrometer at school, but that would be hard to hide.*

Charlie was thinking furiously about how to test a sample if she got one when Sparkle walked into the club. The shock of recognition, together with self-consciousness about *what* she'd been thinking, must have been plain on her face. Tanya leaned close and asked her what was wrong, then she saw Sparkle making her way over to Bill to check in.

"You just be careful, sweetie. Even if Sparkle is innocent as a newborn baby, that guy Frank isn't. Like I told you, I think he's bad news."

Charlie promised to watch out and then decided it was time to work the first few customers coming in. *When I take a break, I'll send Alex an e-mail about this stuff. Damn, what I need is a fucking tricorder, like on* Star Trek.

With that thought, the answer came to her. There was a new gadget at school from a company called MedTox. It was essentially a miniature mass spectrometer. If she could get a sample and snag one of the boxes for just a few minutes, she'd have the answers she needed.

Charlie reached out and squeezed Tanya's hand, mouthed a thank-you at her, then put on her biggest smile and went to work the building crowd. *Now I just have to try and get a sample. How and where? The obvious place to try first is her bag. I have cotton applicator pads in my makeup kit. They're even in a little plastic bag. That should work out perfectly. Now all I have to do is watch for a chance …*

Charlie spent the next couple hours dancing her sets and chatting up the customers. While she was on break, she talked with Diamond and some the other dancers, trying to learn more about Sparkle's party girl rep and her relationship with Frank Spencer. She didn't learn much of anything beyond what Tanya had told her earlier.

Finally, Sparkle disappeared back into the VIP room with a customer. Charlie took one more swallow of her Red Bull and headed downstairs. When she got to the dressing room, there were two other dancers already there. The only thing Charlie could do was make a big show of touching up her makeup, being careful to leave the cotton pads on the countertop, where she could get to them quickly, and then started changing into a new costume.

Just as she was finishing getting dressed, Shadow, the club Goth, and

Elise, a tall brunette with a big smile, finally left the room. Charlie quickly located Sparkle's bag (easy to do because it was covered with sequins) then grabbed the swabs, ran one over the outside, and another over the strap.

She unzipped the bag to run the inside, but what she saw there stopped her cold.

Sitting right before her eyes was a passport. Charlie grabbed for it, opened it up, and saw it was Sparkle's. It looked new. She flipped the pages and came to one with a stamp on it. Looking closer, Charlie could see it was a visa stamp for Brazil! *Shit, this is not good!* Moving as quickly as possible without dropping anything, she reached for her purse, grabbed her phone, and used the camera to take pictures of the passport and stamp. *I'll be damned. Sparkle's real name is Nancy Dawson! I never knew that!*

She ran the third swab around the interior of the gym bag and then folded them into her little plastic bag, doing her best to keep them separated. Charlie had just put them into her own makeup bag when she heard somebody coming down the stairs. Thankfully, it was Amber, a redheaded dancer with creamy skin covered with tattoos, instead of Sparkle.

After exchanging hellos with Amber, Charlie pretended to check her makeup once again and returned to the main room. She was breathing so hard she felt like she'd just finished a long, fast set. She went up to the bar and asked for a glass of water while she got herself under control again. Just as she raised the glass to her lips, she saw Sparkle coming out of the VIP room.

Whew! There was no fucking time to spare, was there? She could be downstairs by now, catching me going through her bag!

Charlie sat down at a table, pulled out her phone, and started composing an e-mail to Alex. As soon as she opened her e-mail app, a message from him popped up. It said he'd had a bad day with his new boss and was going to make an early night of it. He'd call her tomorrow or come by the club.

Charlie quickly pecked out a message that she'd call with info about Spencer and Sparkle tomorrow. It would be best if he didn't come to the club.

That's it for me for tonight! This investigating shit is hard work, and I still have four hours of real work ahead of me.

CHAPTER 17

ALEX WAS SLOW GETTING GOING THE next morning. He'd had a bad night, worrying about Charlie running into trouble while checking out Sparkle at his request. Then there was the chance of Big Mike getting sacked, and on top of that was his unhappiness at having to deal with Drummond on a daily basis. *Put all that together with a dead boss and going to work isn't much fun,* he told himself.

Alex barely made it to the Brass Shack before the official start of shift. The timekeeper gave him a leery expression as he brassed in but didn't say anything. *Good thing she didn't. I'm in no mood to take crap from anybody today, but I bet I'm going to get a boatload anyway.*

Once he got settled at his desk and logged in, Alex discovered that once more the report he needed had not been delivered to his mailbox. After entering yet another trouble ticket, he sent an e-mail to Drummond about the problem. The IM window on Alex's screen said the man was already logged in, but Alex figured the less face time with Drummond the better.

Sure enough, in a couple of minutes a message box popped up. It was from Drummond, and he wanted to see Alex ASAP.

Alex grabbed a notebook and pen and headed to Drummond's office. When he got there, he was surprised to see nobody sitting at the desk. In fact, the office appeared to have been cleaned out.

Oh, crap. I know what this means! Looking down to the far end of the office doublewide, he saw Drummond standing in the door of Big Mike's office. *Damn HQ! They sure didn't waste any time getting rid of Big Mike!*

Drummond didn't even wait for Alex to reach the door before retreating into his office. He was already seated behind Big Mike's desk by the time Alex got there.

"Good morning, Alex. I'm sorry you got in after the formal announcement was made, but as you can see, the head office has relieved Mr. Stuart of his responsibilities here and appointed me to fill the vacancy. I'm sure it will only be temporary. Given the circumstances, I will continue to handle Mr. James' duties as well, so you will continue to report directly to me concerning project status issues. Any questions?"

Alex knew it was pointless to ask why Big Mike had been "relieved." Besides, he'd gotten all he needed to know on that score from Jake. Not quite trusting his voice, he responded with only a negative shake of his head.

"Very well," Drummond went on. "You should know we have been informed via Yankee Power that the Waterford Police Department has decided to close the case of Mr. James' death. While the circumstances are unusual for a suicide, there are no persons unaccounted for who they feel could have been involved. They have also found no *unusual* financial transactions that could provide evidence of any *criminal* activity. So at this point, I believe there should be no further discussion of the matter."

This was Alex's second shock of the day. First Big Mike out, now Walker's case closed! He tried very hard to keep his feelings out of his face as Drummond continued.

"I received your e-mail. Evidently, there was another problem with the consolidated man-hour and cost-summary report again last night?"

Why the hell can't he just say "roll-up report" like everybody else? "Yes, it failed again. I've already created a trouble ticket asking for a rerun." Wanting to prod Drummond a bit, Alex continued. "I thought you were going to talk to corporate IT about it failing."

Drummond obviously liked neither the question nor the tone. "I have spoken to the IT director. He promised me they would track down the problem, but these things can take time. However, he seems to think that there may be some problem on *our* end that is contributing to the issue. Regardless, I trust you will continue to produce the reports as quickly as any *difficulties* allow."

"Certainly," Alex responded. "But in case you don't know the process, let me tell you that all the input to that report is done by the timekeeping staff directly into the systems at corporate via a WAN link. I never touch it, and they get a validation report when they're done. So if there's nothing else, I'll get back to work."

Alex barely waited for an acknowledgment from Drummond before he got up and left. When he got to his desk, he realized he'd never turned on his phone after charging it. As soon as it was powered up, it vibrated. He sat down, took a few deep breaths before he checked it, and immediately saw an e-mail from Charlie.

As he read it, Alex couldn't believe the coup Charlie had pulled off the night before. She related her talk with Tanya and what she found in Sparkle's bag. The photos of the passport were attached too. The e-mail ended with a promise to get the samples into the MedTox device before she had to leave for the club that afternoon.

If the meth samples match what killed Walker, would that be enough to get the authorities to reopen the case? I doubt it. Cops don't like being shown they missed something. Hell, nobody does!

Alex composed a quick reply to Charlie, praising her for her discoveries. An idea popped into his mind, and before sending it, he turned to his computer to quickly check a couple of websites. *So the weather tomorrow is clear and cold and the airplane is available.* Going back to the phone, he tacked on another sentence. "Weather is good tomorrow and plane is free. Let's play hooky and go flying, okay?" Then he sent it off and buckled down to getting the morning report done.

Once he'd inputted all the data he had, he took a moment to put a sick-leave request into the system; no way he'd get vacation time with notice this short. It came back approved even before the new roll-up report showed up in his box.

Charlie was on her way to the forensics lab when the mail from Alex popped up. She smiled at the "atta girl" he gave her and then read the final sentence with surprise. *Well, why not? I busted my ass during midterms and I need a break. Maybe I can blow off my sociology class tomorrow afternoon.*

The forensics lab had an equipment cage that was pretty much the same sort of thing you'd find at a gym. This one, however, held lots more interesting stuff than basketballs and baseball bats. She went up to the window and asked the work-study student inside the cage for a MedTox unit. He asked no questions—there was no reason to. She handed over her student ID, signed out the box, and went to a lab bench.

It took only a few minutes for her to reread the preparation and operations instructions. The unit was designed to be used in the field so it was simple to use. In just a few minutes, she had a sample prepared and in the machine. Charlie hit the START button and waited, not very patiently, for the cycle to finish. It took about fifteen minutes.

The unit had both an LCD screen and a printer. One quick look at the screen was all it took for her to barely suppress a yell of triumph and not jump up and down in joy. *They match! The swabs from Sparkle's bag and the exemplar from the body match! Sparkle* must *have had something to do with Walker's death!*

She hit the PRINT button, waited for the report to pop out, and then stuck the printout in her bag, all the while debating whether to tell Alex right away or wait until tomorrow. She made the simultaneous decision to ditch class to go flying with Alex and to wait until she saw him to give him the details.

She quickly cleaned up from the test, returned the machine, and reclaimed her ID card. Going to her next class was the last thing she wanted to do, but she told herself to settle down. She headed off to her physics lecture.

After taking a seat in the lecture hall, she pulled out her phone and sent an e-mail to Alex. She wrote, "Got results. Tell u tomorrow. See u @ 2 at ur place."

While Charlie was running her samples, Alex was watching his computer screen for an e-mail with the roll-up report data. Though he didn't know it, it showed up just as Charlie was celebrating her results. He was inputting the necessary figures into his own report when his phone buzzed. Alex started to reach for it when he noticed that the re-rack building scope had changed yet again. *What the hell is going on now? The new scope has been cut just about in half!*

Instead of going to Drummond to ask why, he decided to call Jake and ask him if he knew what was going on. Since he had Jake on speed dial on his cell, Alex used that instead of the office line. Before placing the call, he saw that Charlie had accepted his invitation for tomorrow. Alex pushed Jake's number and his friend answered quickly. "Hey, Alex. What's up?"

"A couple things, Jake. First, you were right about Big Mike. He was gone before I even got in this morning. Drummond's sitting in his office now."

"Damn, that sucks. I'm really sorry to hear that, Alex. I was pretty sure it was coming down the pike, but that doesn't help."

"Yeah, I know what you mean. The other thing is this change in scope to the re-rack building. Any idea what's going on there? I don't want to ask Drummond, and the project managers are out in the field right now."

Jake gave a snort and replied, "Management has decided, in its infinite wisdom, that we don't need the re-rack building after all. You guys aren't going to move it. The scope change you have is to disassemble the whole damn thing! To meet the EPA requirements, we also have to demolish the cast wall. After that, we have to get a specialty restoration company to come in and replant the area."

Alex couldn't believe his ears. "You can't be serious! You people have poured a ton of money into that building and you had a reason for the project, didn't you?"

"It's just been too big a boondoggle. The only good thing about the whole snafu is that management is coming down on Frank Spencer like a ton of bricks for screwing it up. He's out on his ass. I don't know if he'll be fired or get a chance to retire. Anyway, he's through."

Alex's mind immediately turned to the passport that Charlie had found the night before. *Damn it. I bet they're both going to bolt!*

"Jake, hang on. I have to log into my personal e-mail on my computer." Putting the phone down, Alex frantically opened a new Firefox window and hit the bookmark for his e-mail account. He selected Charlie's e-mail, hit forward, and picked Jake's address.

Alex picked up his phone again and told Jake, "I sent an e-mail to your phone. Let me know when you get it. You need to read it right now. Got it?"

"Not yet, Alex. Jesus, it's not a local connection we're using here. What's so secret you can't just tell me?"

"You'll see when you get it. Is it there?"

"Damn it, keep your pants on … Yeah, it's here. Call you right back after I look at it."

Alex sat fuming at his desk, swearing at the limitations of some smart phones, until Jake called him back.

"Goddamn it, Alex. Charlie's a bloody genius! Beauty, brains, and guts in one package. Wait, what's with this passport stuff?"

"Think, buddy, think. Who's this girl involved with?"

"Oh crap!" Jake exclaimed. "If she's getting ready to run, she's probably going with Spencer! If he did kill Walker, then he may be gone forever, right?"

"That's what I'm thinking. Charlie accepted my offer to go flying tomorrow. I'll let you know what she's got to say. If you hear anything new, let me know, will you please?"

Jake's reply was a fervent "You bet your ass I will!" And then Alex killed the call.

The only thing to do was to continue plugging away at his morning report, even though it was almost noon now. Alex finished it, sent it to the printer, and then took it to Drummond's office. Luckily, he was already involved in another meeting so Alex just dropped it on his desk and backed out.

It was a long afternoon. Keeping his mind on the paper coming across his desk was almost impossible. Lunch was a welcome break and he got to commiserate with the project supes about Big Mike's firing. Just about everybody thought it was bullshit.

A couple of support tickets came in to break his preoccupation with Charlie's and Jake's news plus his anxiety about the news she'd give him tomorrow. The day finally came to an end and he headed home.

The evening was, in its own way, worse than work. He checked the weather for the next day, flew a few approaches on Microsoft Flight Simulator just for practice, and chewed his nails a lot. Dinner was more soup. The only saving grace was it didn't matter that it was after one in the morning when he fell asleep, because he didn't have to get up at the crack of dawn to go to work.

CHAPTER 18

IT WAS TEN O'CLOCK WHEN ENOUGH sunlight finally sneaked its way into the bedroom to wake Alex from his troubled sleep. The night had been full of dreams about Walker, Frank Spencer, and Sparkle. He woke with a start and virtually the first thought to penetrate his sleep-sodden brain was *We still can't place the son of a bitch at the scene of the crime!*

Feelings of frustration and dissatisfaction stayed with him all morning. He walked over to the Country Kitchen for breakfast, lingering over coffee and the New London *Day*. Once back in his apartment, Alex searched Monster.com for any jobs that would get him the hell out of Connecticut but didn't find much. After sending out a few résumés, it hit him that leaving Connecticut also meant leaving behind Charlie. *Damn it, Alex. The girl has her own life to lead. She graduates this spring and she's not going to hang around for an old fart like you!*

As it got closer to two o'clock, he started checking the weather. He also called the airport to make sure that there were no problems caused by the recent storm, like downed power lines or trees. When lunchtime rolled around, he made himself a peanut butter sandwich and settled down to his last resort: TCM. This time it was an old John Wayne flick, *Island in the Sky*, about a WWII transport plane crashing in the Canadian wilderness.

Charlie, thank God, showed up right on time. The light, quick steps on the stairs told him who his visitor was. He was at the door before she could even knock. He swept her off her feet in an exuberant hug, turned, and plopped her back down inside the apartment.

The two of them exchanged grins for a couple of seconds, and then

Charlie slid one hand up to the back of Alex's head and pulled his face down to hers. Before Alex even realized what was happening, Charlie's lips were warm on his. After an instant of doubt, he tightened his arms around her body and gave all he had to that deep, lingering kiss.

When they finally came up for air, they stood there, foreheads touching, happy to be together again. They didn't stay like that for long because Charlie pushed him back to arm's length so she could watch his face as she spoke.

"Alex, I've got to tell you. The chemical composition of the swabs I took from Sparkle's bag and the meth in Walker's body match! They're identical! What do you think about that? I've been dying to see the look on your face when I told you!"

Alex didn't let Charlie down. His expression started out as dumfounded, turned happy, and then changed to troubled. He told her, "That's incredibly good information, but it still doesn't help us put either of them in the plant. The security systems say no and the cops have given up. Since they can't find anybody with opportunity or any funky financial transactions, they're closing the case."

Charlie's eyes went wide at that news. "They can't do that! Don't you think we have enough new evidence to get the case reopened?"

Alex shook his head and told her, "They'll say maybe they used the same dealer, or maybe that Sparkle *is* a dealer, but that's not going be enough for them to reopen the case."

"So what now?" Charlie asked.

"Now we go flying and forget this crap for a while. Let me get my stuff and we'll get a move on." Alex put on his coat and hat and then reached for his phone before putting on his gloves.

"What are you doing?" Charlie asked.

"It's cold out there and the hangar isn't heated. The airplane has an engine heater and we have a remote control gadget that lets us turn it on."

Like a thunderclap, the final piece of the damning puzzle fell into place. Alex actually felt dizzy for a second. The emotions on his face must have been manifest, because Charlie started demanding to know what was wrong.

"I think I know how Spencer, and maybe Sparkle, got into the plant without going through security! Hang on a minute."

Ignoring Charlie's demands to know how, Alex went back into the bedroom and grabbed his Canon Rebel digital camera. He brought it back into the kitchen and handed it to Charlie. "Do you know how to use this?" he asked her.

"I've never used this model, but I know how to shoot. I'll fiddle with it while we're driving. Alex, how did he do it and why do we need the camera?"

"You held off telling me about the samples until this morning," he told her with a huge grin splitting his beard, "so I'm going to make you wait to find out what just hit me. Actually, it will make more sense from the air. Come on. Let's move it."

Charlie still wasn't happy to be kept in the dark about the big break, but she could tell she wasn't going to get anything more out of Alex. They got in the truck and headed for the airport. Charlie made sure the camera was set to auto mode and she knew where the zoom and shutter buttons were. Alex told her that was all she'd need.

The drive to the airport only took about twenty minutes. After parking the truck next to his hangar, Alex unlocked a side door and gestured for Charlie to go on in. He followed and then hit a light switch to illuminate the interior. Even though it wasn't heated, the hangar kept the wind off, and that meant something on a cold day like today.

When Alex came in, Charlie was standing there looking at the airplane. "Honey, it's even prettier than the picture you showed me. This airplane is almost forty years old?"

"Amazing what a new paint job can do, isn't it? It's the original design but new colors. Remind me to show you what it used to look like sometime."

Despite being in a dreadful hurry to prove his theory, Alex forced himself to go through his usual methodical and thorough preflight checks. He opened the pilot's door, checked the fuel and tachometer hours, and entered it all in the time sheet. He grabbed a laminated card from one of the seat pockets and handed it to Charlie. "You've been in little airplanes before, right?" When she nodded yes, he told her, "Then I'm not going to go into a lot of details right now about how stuff works. Read that, will you please?" Then he went systematically around the airplane making sure, as one of his instructors had taught him years ago, that there was nothing hanging and nothing dripping.

"Alex, this is like the cards they have in the seat pockets of airliners, but it's for this plane. Are you pulling my leg?"

"Nope. The regs say we have to tell you the same stuff the big boys do. I found that online last year and printed it out. Neat, huh?"

"If you say so. Are we almost ready?" Charlie asked.

"Almost. Stand clear of the hangar doors."

Alex pushed a control button on the hangar wall and the door began to fold in the middle. While this was happening, he put a tow bar on the nose wheel while saying to Charlie, "Could you go outside please, and watch the wingtips? I don't want to knock them on the other planes or the sides of the hangar."

Charlie moved to where she could see both wings and shouted to him, "How are you going to get it out? You're not just going to pull it, are you?"

Bending down to grab the bar, Alex yelled back "Yes! It weighs less than your hatchback! It really isn't that hard to move."

Almost as soon as he finished his explanation, the airplane was out in sunlight. Since he was in a hurry and it would be a short flight, Alex didn't even bother to close the hangar door. Removing the tow bar, he placed it on the floor behind the front seats then went around to help Charlie get in and settled.

As he made sure her seat belt and shoulder harness were secure, Alex told her, "Honey, I'm sorry, but this isn't going to be a really fun flight. I want to get us to where we can take pictures, and I can show you how the SOB did it. This headset is for you. There's an intercom so we can talk to each other without shouting." He handed her the green David Clark headset, and after she put it on, he told her, "Get the microphone right by the corner of your mouth. That's great."

Alex closed her door and walked quickly to the left side of the airplane. He climbed in, shut his door, adjusted the seat and restraints, and then put on his own headset. With everything set, he took the checklist from the door pocket on his side and started to run through it. His hands moved purposefully across the controls, setting them to start the engine. Cardinals have little "wing" windows like you find in older cars. Alex cranked his open and yelled, "Clear!" as loud as he could, and turned the key to start. One, two, three, four blades of the propeller went by, and then the engine caught. When it was idling smoothly, he turned his attention back to Charlie.

"Can you hear me now?" he spoke into the microphone while looking at Charlie.

"Yes, I can. Are you sure you know what you're doing?" she asked him.

"Hundreds and hundreds of flights and the takeoffs and landings are equal. No sweat, honey." Then he keyed the mic button under his finger and announced, "Waterford traffic, Cardinal 29849 taxiing for departure runway three-two, Waterford." Simultaneously, he eased the throttle forward and they began to move.

He stopped the airplane between the two runways to do his engine check. "It's going to get a little loud," he told Charlie. He checked the magnetos and did the rest of the pre-takeoff checklist. As he took a good look around for other airplanes, he keyed the mic and spoke again. "Waterford traffic, Cardinal 849 back-taxiing runway three-two for departure." Giving it more throttle, he turned right down the runway, turned around at the far end, and turned to look at Charlie. "You ready?"

She nodded yes.

"Okay, time to commit aviation!" Then he keyed the mic once more and said, "Waterford traffic, Cardinal 849 departing runway three-two, straight out departure." He pushed the throttle all the way in.

In the cool air, the airplane virtually jumped forward, and in only a few seconds, it was at flying speed. Alex trimmed for a seventy-five knot climb and spoke to Charlie again. "Please keep your eyes open for other airplanes, honey. Let me know if you see any."

"Will you please tell me what we're going to do?" demanded Charlie, obviously frustrated.

"Give me a second to level off." They'd already reached 1,750 feet. They needed to be that high to stay out of trouble while overflying the nature sanctuary next to Osprey Point but low enough for the photos he wanted to take. He turned the airplane to the west and started talking to Charlie while keeping his eyes outside.

"We're going to come back along the shore and you're going to take pictures of the plant. Look for a yellow building with a white roof along the northern perimeter road, just south of the switchyard. Got that?"

"I think so, but aren't you breaking some laws by flying that close to the plant? I thought after 9/11 that was illegal?"

Alex shook his head. "No, it's not. Nuke plants were completely out-of-bounds for a while, even though they wouldn't tell pilots where they were so we could avoid them! Now the rule is to 'not circle so as to loiter' near them. We'll make one pass and head home."

"Just so I'm sure, what's a switchyard look like?" Charlie asked.

As he started to turn the plane south, Alex said, "Like a big electrical substation. Lots of gray towers, insulators, and wires."

"Okay. You want close-ups or what?"

"A mix," Alex told her. "Zoom in and out and don't worry about how many. There's a fresh sixty-four-gigabyte memory card in there."

They had almost reached the shoreline, so Alex turned again so they would be passing far enough north of the plant to give Charlie an angle to shoot.

"See the big red and white stack out ahead of us? That's the plant. What we're looking for is to the left of that."

Charlie peered over the glare shield and spotted the stack. She turned her attention to the camera, made sure it was on and zoomed out for a wide view to start. "Why don't we just look at Google Earth?" she asked him.

"Good idea, but the building we're looking for is brand new. It won't show up yet. Can you see the switchyard now and that white roof to the right of it?"

Charlie strained her eyes to see what he was talking about and then ducked her head to look through the side window. There it was! "I got it!" she said.

"Great. I'm going to slow down a little to give you more time. Start shooting anytime. Zoom in and out!" Alex told her.

"I heard you the first time. Can you turn a little so I can see better?"

Alex decided he'd have to slip the airplane to give her a good view. He warned, "The airplane's going to feel like it's going sideways. Don't worry. It's under control." Then he dropped the right wing while adding in some left rudder. Cessna Cardinals have no wing struts so Charlie had an unobstructed view now.

Still wondering what the hell this was all about, Charlie feverishly snapped pictures while zooming in and out. By the time the plant was too far behind them for her to get the building framed, she had fired off fifty shots.

"So what now?" she asked.

"Let's get back on the ground and I'll tell you," Alex responded.

"No! I want to know now!"

"Okay, let me turn away and climb a little. Then I'll tell you."

After steadying on a northerly course and climbing to 2,500 feet, Alex set the autopilot to keep the plane level and started to explain. "That building is called the re-rack building. Frank Spencer was the Yankee Power project manager for it until yesterday. He screwed it up from day one. There have been cost overruns like you can't believe, and I found out yesterday that he missed that the damn thing is built on wetlands. EPA never gave Yankee Power a permit to build there, so the whole thing has to come down.

"Scroll back and look at the shots you took. See the end of the building that's right up against the fence? There are actually gates there to let a semi back in far enough for an overhead crane to pick up containers of fuel rods and load them onto the truck. The crane can extend *over* the fence because the full length of the trailer can't go into the building when it's full of containers.

"It came to me when I hit the remote control for the aircraft heater on my phone. My guess is that Spencer has rigged a remote control to the crane and doors. The thing is actually run from a wireless remote control so maybe he just ordered two and rigged an interface for the doors. Either way, I'm sure he can open the doors, extend the crane, drop the hook, and then hoist himself right up over the fence and into the plant. *That's* how he got into the plant to kill Walker!"

Alex had been looking out the windshield and scanning for other traffic while giving Charlie the scoop on his theory. When he finished, he turned to look at her. Her face seemed to be nothing but wide eyes and arched eyebrows, her mouth a tight little O. Charlie seemed to be trying to get words out. It took her a few moments to get her voice working again.

"Alex, you've got it! Oh my God, you've got it. We've both been pounding our heads against this wall for *days* and you figured it out. You're the man!"

Alex smiled at her and said, "Thanks, honey. Now all we have to do is figure out how to catch the bastard. The cops have closed the case, so now I have to figure out some way to make him come to me. I think I know how to do that too."

"What do you mean *come to you*? We have enough to open the case back up. Call the police or the FBI!"

Alex shook his head as he hit the autopilot disconnect and headed back for Waterford. "There's still no financial connection. I'm still in the dark about that myself, and without that, the cops won't touch it. But since there has to be one, I think I can use that to lure him in."

Charlie continued to protest and Alex continued to insist that he, with help from Jake, could handle the situation. "I need you to go to work as usual and keep an eye on Sparkle. I'll send you an app you may need later. Think you can take Sparkle down if you need to?"

Those final words shocked Charlie to her core. "What do you mean? What do you want me to do?"

"I'm going to need you to keep her in one spot once I give you a call. The app is a call recording one Jake came up with so we could record telephone weather briefings. It's not strictly legal, but it works."

"You'll have your buddy Jake to help you? You promise you won't get yourself killed?"

"I promise. Now let me get this thing on the ground and put away so I can get the rest of this in motion."

CHAPTER 19

THE LANDING BACK AT WATERFORD WAS smooth enough to impress Charlie and Alex quickly got the airplane put away. They drove back to his apartment, Alex thinking furiously about the details of a plan to trap Spencer. As soon as he parked the truck behind his apartment, Alex pulled out his phone and called Jake.

"Alex, how was the flying?" his friend asked as he answered.

"It was great, but that's not why I'm calling. I need you to get your tail over here, ASAP. Tell the boss you're sick, you have a toothache—I don't care. Get over here, quick as you can."

"What's up, brother? You in some kind of trouble?"

"No, but Spencer is. Get over here, like yesterday." Alex disconnected before Jake could even reply.

Charlie looked at Alex, worry all over her pretty face. "What are you going to do?"

"I haven't got all the details worked out yet. Please, Charlie, let me hash out some ideas with Jake and I'll let you know."

He took a deep breath and then looked her right in the eyes as he told her, "It's asking a lot, I know. I really don't have any right to ask you to get involved in this. If you don't want to help, I'll understand. You've done enough already."

Charlie reached out and grabbed him around the neck. Once again, she pulled his face to hers and kissed him. "I don't know what it is about you. Maybe you are a white knight with an airplane instead of a horse, but whatever it is, I'm in."

Alex hugged her as well as he could in the confines of the Ranger's cab. "Thank you, Charlie. Thanks a lot. One way or another, this should be over by tomorrow night and we can go from there, okay?"

"Just make sure that *you* come out of this in one piece! You hear me?"

"I hear you. Let's get you on your way while I get set up for Jake."

After Charlie had driven off, Alex went upstairs and put the memory card into his computer so he could show Jake the pictures to back up his theory. Soon, he heard heavy feet coming up the stairs to his apartment. He opened the door before his best buddy could knock and asked him in.

"Throw your coat anywhere. Want some coffee?" Alex asked.

"Not the crap you drink. But since I knew I was coming to the Temple of the Coffee Heathens, I brought some Jamaica Blue along for us. Actually, move your tail out of the way and *I'll* make it!"

As far as Alex was concerned, Jake was a coffee snob of the first order. But if it was going make him happy to have his own coffee, Alex wasn't going to argue.

Alex asked about Jake's wife and brother-in-law while the coffee was dripping and got out the mugs, cream, and sugar. No artificial sweeteners were allowed in Jamaica Blue.

After they were settled at the kitchen table, Alex brought up the reason he asked his friend here rather than talking to him at the plant. "Jake, I need your help, and I know you're going to hate what I'm asking you to do. I'm certain Frank Spencer killed Walker, but the cops have it down as an accidental OD and they don't want to hear anything else. They've closed the case, period."

"Alex, you've been obsessed with your boss's death since day one. If the cops are so sure, why don't you give it up?"

"I can't, and I'll tell you why." Alex quickly filled in his friend on his idea of how Spencer had gotten access via the re-rack building. He pulled up the aerial shots on his big monitor to back up the theory. Then he reiterated Spencer's relationship with Sparkle from Rosie's, emphasizing the match between the meth in Sparkle's bag and the stuff used to kill Walker. Then he went on to theorize about the cost overruns on the re-rack building and Spencer's hand in running up the tab.

As Alex spoke, Jake's expression ran the gamut from impatient exasperation to interest to disbelief, ending up with puzzlement.

"How do you figure the girl fits in? How can she soak up that much change?" he asked. "How's the money getting out of YP to Spencer? The cops never found any link."

"Because in addition to the big tips and expensive gifts, Spencer's been paying for her meth habit. The drugs that killed Walker were hers! That can't account for all the money, but my guess is the rest is tucked away somewhere so he can retire someplace warm and sunny with his sweetie pie. As to how the money gets moved, I think I have that figured out too. I have to do some checking at work tomorrow."

Jake was starting to believe his friend, but he still wasn't sure playing Watson to Alex's Holmes was the way to go. "Why don't you go to management with this? Hell, I'll take it my boss if you want."

Alex shook his head and replied, "Because Yankee Power already has a Trippler guy holding the bag for the fraud. That makes them victims and gets them off easy with the PUC *and* their shareholders. Big Mike got canned for this and the new head honcho doesn't want waves. He wants the whole thing under the rug and work back to normal."

Jake sat back and gave his friend a long, hard look. He thought back to all the years they'd known each other, since junior high, and how many scrapes they'd survived together. He trusted this guy with his life, but he still couldn't grasp what his friend was telling him.

"Alex," he finally said, "you're not shitting me on this, are you? You really believe Spencer murdered Walker."

Leaning forward in his chair, arms on the table, Alex tried to muster as much sincerity as he could and shove it into every word he spoke. "Brother, I *am* serious. We've known each other for twenty-four years, and if I didn't believe this bastard was a killer, I would not ask you to put your ass on the line. You know that."

Jake stared down at his hands, fingers splayed out on the kitchen table. His mind was racing, reviewing everything his friend had told him. After thirty seconds, which seemed a lot longer to Alex, he looked up at his best friend and spoke the words Alex needed to hear. "Okay, I'm in. What do you need?"

Alex let out a huge sigh of relief while a big smile split his bearded face, something nobody had seen recently. "I need you to hack two systems for me. The first is easy. Hell, you might even have access already."

"What system?" Jake asked.

"The Health Physics data base. I need to know every time in the last few months that Spencer went through the Unit III construction rad portal."

"Okay, that one's easy. You're right. I do have access to that one so I can track worker exposure during outages. What's the other one?"

"You'll hate the next one, and you'll wish you never agreed to this. I need you to hack WATCHDOG." He knew Jake wasn't going to like this, and he watched warily for Jake's response.

The color just drained out of Jake's ruddy face. "You are not even supposed to *know* that name! It's the most secure and only secret system in the whole fucking plant! How the *hell* did you find out about that?"

"Does it matter? I know, and I know it will give us the answers we need."

Jake was still fuming about the security breach and demanded, "And just what the fuck does that mean? Hacking into that system means jail, not just getting fired and blacklisted if we get caught! Hell, *when* we get caught!"

Alex shot back, "Spencer has an alibi; he said he wasn't in the plant the night Walker died. WATCHDOG records who goes through every monitored door and gate. It keeps track of every motion sensor trip and power fluctuation. Jake, I *know* Spencer killed Walker. He *had* to be in the plant to do it. I think I've figured out how he got around perimeter security, but I'm betting nobody—not him, YP, or the cops—was smart enough to realize he still had to go through the Unit III construction radiation portal to get to the Trippler offices. When we find a rad detector hit when he's not supposed to be in the plant, we've got his ass."

Alex explained again the revelation that had come to him while getting ready for his flight with Charlie and pointed again to the aerial photos of the plant they'd taken. Jake had never been a good poker player and the reason why showed on his face as he listened again to Alex's explanation. His expression evolved from anger to disbelief to grim resolution. "Okay, that all makes sense," he responded. "But don't you have enough to get the cops to change their minds?"

"I don't think so," replied Alex. "I have an idea on how to deal with that too. It will call for some close timing and some Web programming on your part, but I think we can handle it."

Alex proceeded to outline his plan to his friend. When he was finished, Jake blurted, "You are out of your frigging mind! This is too damn much! You could get killed!"

Alex coolly replied, "I'm betting not. I think I've got an ace in the hole he won't take into account. At least I hope so. Meanwhile, let's get to work."

It took five hours and two pots of coffee to work out the details, including the specs for hacks and programming changes Jake needed to do. When they finished, Jake pushed back from the table, closed his red eyes, dug his palms into them, and rubbed hard enough to see flashes in the darkness.

"Can you think of *anything* else that might help?" Alex asked his friend.

"Not right now," Jake replied. "This is enough to keep me busy all night, especially since I have to do it from home. The only reason this can work is the fact that the site I need to get to is secured from *outside* attacks and I'll be working via the VPN, which is *inside* the extra security. If I don't get caught right away, we should be safe for at least a week before the next security audit."

"That's more than be enough time," Alex assured him. "Let me know how you're doing. Obviously, you'll need to be discrete about it."

"You bet your ass I'll be discrete," Jake retorted. "Just don't drop the goddamn ball on your end, old buddy."

One quick pit stop and Jake was on his way out. With the door already open, he turned to Alex and asked him one last time, "Are you sure you want to go through with this? I might end up out of a job and maybe in jail. You could get killed."

Alex gave a slow, sure nod. "I know. Yes, this is something I've got to do. I can't tell you how much it means to have you with me on this."

"Don't get sentimental on me, not now. Maybe after we're done."

The two friends went into a quick bear hug, and then Jake was on his way. Alex watched him go down the stairs and get into his car. As he closed the door, he thought, *If we're* both *around after it's all done.* Then he sat down at his computer to tell Charlie that Jake had joined the operation.

Alex spent the night going over his plan, trying to find holes to plug. He had tried to keep it as simple as possible and couldn't think of any changes to make. After a restless night, he got up early for work. He needed to check some things out before Drummond got in.

Once he was in his office, the first thing he did was to pull out a set of re-rack plans from the project supervisor's files. He quickly confirmed the overhead crane had sufficient reach to make it over the fence. It was also mounted high enough above the ground to keep the motion sensors from triggering. *Okay, that's confirmed.*

The next thing he did was use his admin credentials to look at two different sets of reports. One was the historical roll-up report. The other was a disbursing report that showed, by job, what was actually going into and (more importantly) out of Trippler's accounts. *They don't match! Everybody was looking at how money could get diverted from YP! They never stopped to think that it was being stolen from Trippler!*

He e-mailed his findings to Jake, telling him to be near the re-rack building before eight o'clock that night. Alex expected Spencer to use that entry method one last time, and Jake was to disable the crane after Spencer had left the area, then move to Unit III near the MAP. Jake acknowledged the instructions, told Alex he was an idiot, and confirmed his programming was done and tested as far as it could be. He also reported the vital information that there were numerous times when Spencer's key card was registered going through the Unit III radiation checkpoint when WATCHDOG showed he wasn't in the plant. One of those hits was the night Walker was murdered.

Now Alex e-mailed Charlie, telling her she needed to get Sparkle isolated just after eight, have her phone dialed into his, and have the recording app on. She responded much as Jake did.

The day dragged on and on, but finally the critical time came. Alex looked up Frank Spencer's office number, punched it into his cell phone, and then went outside to make the call unheard.

"Frank Spencer, who is this?" came the raspy, unmistakable voice.

"Spencer, it's Alex Strong from Trippler. I need to talk to you."

"About what? If you haven't heard the happy news, I'm outta here at the end of the week. My projects have already been turned over."

Mustering as calm a tone as he could, Alex continued. "This is about the re-rack building, Spencer. I know that you've been siphoning money off, and I know you killed Walker. No skin off my nose either way, but you've made a pile of money off this scam, and I want some of it."

"What the fuck are you talking about? I had nothing to do with that jerk-off's death!"

"Don't try and kid me, Spencer. I know about you and your girlfriend. I know you're getting ready to leave the country. Come to Walker's old office at eight tonight, or I go to the cops tomorrow."

Alex killed the call. *The bait is out there. Let's see if I can set the hook!*

Chapter 20

THE NEXT FEW HOURS WERE TORTURE for Alex. He couldn't leave the plant because WATCHDOG wouldn't let him back in after his assigned hours. Staying late didn't matter to the security systems. However, he did have to brass-out at his normal time. He pretended to forget something and went back to the offices. There he made a big show of tearing down a PC and fiddling with it until everybody was gone. Then he started biting his nails as the time crept closer to eight. He confirmed Jake's and Charlie's instructions and tried to wait as calmly as he could. Just before the appointed hour, he went into Walker's old office and placed a call to Charlie. He left the phone on, volume turned down, and slipped it into his shirt pocket. He'd made sure earlier it had a full charge.

Just a couple of minutes before eight, he heard the outside door open and close, then the slow and heavy footsteps of somebody walking slowly but heavily toward the office.

In just a few seconds, Spencer stood in the door, looking very big and menacing.

Alex stood and then said, "Glad you could make it, Frank. I didn't really want to call the cops on you."

"And what have you got to tell them, you geek bastard?"

"That I know how you got into the plant to kill Walker. You used the remote control on the crane at the re-rack building, didn't you? That, and one you built to open the doors. Nice job, by the way."

Spencer was getting redder by the moment, and Alex knew he was on the right track. "Walker must have found out the money from the re-rack project was being laundered through Trippler, right? He figured you had to be making all the mistakes on the project to drive up costs and get more money into your pocket, so he called you about it and wanted to talk. He had no idea of your sweetie at the club and your plans to run away together, so he didn't know how desperate his discoveries had made you. Tell me: did you kill him by yourself? Or did your girlfriend ride you piggy-back up the crane and shoot meth up his nose while your wrapped those big, strong arms of yours around him? With winter coats to pad things, there wouldn't be any bruising, would there, Spencer?"

"You think you're so damn smart, don't you? Got it all figured out. Well, I killed Walker and got away with it, so why not you too? Since we're all set to leave, I'll do this one myself, the hard way. We'll be out of the country before they find your body, jackass."

Spencer advanced on Alex, hands flexing, his face pale for once. As he started to close in, he jumped in surprise as, of all things, his cell phone rang! As the ring tone played out, a worried look flashed across his face.

"Better answer that, Frank. Your girlfriend has something important to tell you." Alex's voice was a lot calmer than he felt.

Keeping himself between Alex and the door, Spencer slipped a hand to his back pocket and removed his phone.

"Put it on speaker, Frank. I'd like to hear what Sparkle—or should I call her Nancy?—has to say."

Now it was worry on Spencer's face—no doubt about it. There was some surprise, perhaps, mixed in too, because Alex knew Sparkle's real name.

He pushed the speakerphone button. "Hello, honey, is that you?"

"Frankie!" a panicked voice came over the phone. "Frankie, they know! That bitch Charlie has got me—" The voice turned into a muffled scream. Then Charlie's voice picked up.

"Hi, Frankie. It's your worst nightmare calling. I've got your girl toy down in the dressing room of the club. Alex's phone is active too, and I've heard everything. What's more, he gave me this neat little app to record calls, both in and out. I've got everything on my phone, and Alex has it on his too. You'd better do what he tells you."

Panic was all over Spencer by the time Charlie finished; the blotchy red was starting to show. "What the fuck do you want?" he shouted at Alex.

"I want you to turn around and leave," Alex replied. "Here's your one shot to go rescue your girlfriend. Leave me alone, keep your phone turned on so Charlie can hear I'm okay, and go get her. Oh, I have to warn you that a friend of mine has disabled the crane on the re-rack building. You're going to have to go out by the MAP. Just thought you might want to know that."

It was obvious that Spencer was torn between killing Alex where he stood and going after the woman who obsessed him. All the plans, all the hopes for his future with the *femme fatale* who had bewitched him, went running through his mind like a DVR on fast-forward.

"You'll just call the cops the moment I leave!" he said harshly.

"Not me, not Charlie. My number one goal is clearing Walker's name. The recordings, along with the financial data I've got, will do that. Keep your girl on the line and you'll know if something happens. Last chance, Spencer. Take it and run."

Spencer made his decision. He turned and ran out of the office, feet pounding on the flimsy floor. Alex heard the outer door slam open as Spencer bolted for freedom.

Alex picked up his phone and spoke into it. "He's out, Charlie. I've got to call Jake. Hang tight, honey."

"Be careful, sweetie. I've got this piece of trash wrapped up."

Alex hit disconnect then speed-dialed Jake's phone. When Jake answered, he told him, "Spencer's on his way, brother. Get him!"

Hidden in the shadow cast by Unit III, Jake replied, "Looking. Yeah, there he is. Stand by."

Jake saw Spencer run up close to the exit and slowed to a walk, not wanting to appear out of the ordinary. Watching closely, Jake poised a fingertip over one of the Easter Egg links he had created on the plant control Web page.

Spencer reached the door, pulled it open, and went inside, still trying to slow down and look normal. The instant the outside door closed, Jake's finger fell onto the screen. An eye blink later, no more, the entire plant erupted with horns, sirens, and flashing red lights. WATCHDOG had just ordered a security shutdown of the entire plant. Every door controlled by the system was locked. Spencer was trapped at the exit turnstile. Now the question was how long it would last before Security Central reset the system.

As soon as he heard the sirens go, Alex left Trippler's offices and headed for the MAP at a dead run. A WATCHDOG shutdown also triggered an alarm at the Waterford PD and he could already hear sirens on Rope Ferry Road.

He caught up with Jake outside the MAP. "Glad to see you're still alive, brother," Jake greeted him. "I was getting worried there."

Alex's only response was a breathless "Me too."

Through the glass doors, they could see Spencer struggling against the steel bars of the turnstile. Trapped like the rat he was, he still fought to get out. He turned to try the glass doors, saw Alex and Jake outside, and threw himself against them in his rage. Being sturdier than the standard mall door, nothing gave way.

"Let me out of here, you bastards!" he shouted. "Let me out or I'll kill you both!"

A security guard wearing captain's railroad tracks appeared, obviously confused about the shutdown but following protocol. "You two have to go back to your work areas until we're clear," he said to them both. Then he noticed that Alex was wearing a Trippler badge. "And you're not even supposed to be here! What the hell is going on?"

Jake flashed his YP badge. The bright gold stripe around the edge caught the guard's attention. It denoted a high-value Yankee Power employee.

"You're the watch commander?" Jake asked. The man nodded. "This is a police matter, captain," Jake informed the guard. "Listen to the recording this guy has of the man in the airlock." He gestured at Alex.

Alex hit play, and in a few seconds, Spencer's confession was playing over the speakerphone. The captain stopped looking pissed-off and started to look grim. Reaching for his walkie-talkie, he keyed it up and made a call. "MAP Control, this is supervisor 3. When the doors release, detain the guy in the airlock. Nondeadly force is authorized. Hold for PD." As the acknowledgment came through, two WPD squad cars screeched to a halt in front of the MAP, blue lights flashing.

With a *clunk* they could hear from outside, the locks on the heavy turnstile released. Three husky security guards tackled Spencer as he pushed through the bars, still screaming and foaming at the mouth.

A few seconds later, speakers all over the plant started blaring, "Security system fault! No intruder! All clear! Repeat, all clear!" The lockdown had given them just seconds more than they needed to trap Spencer.

Alex and Jake were directed out of the secure area by the watch commander. Inside the MAP stood two Waterford PD officers. One of them was a sergeant who demanded to know what the hell was going on.

The guard captain explained the guy on the floor, now sobbing uncontrollably, was a murder suspect and pointed to Alex. "Better listen to what he's got," the guard told the sergeant.

Suspicion and anger were radiating from the policeman. Alex and Jake ID'd themselves, and then Alex started to explain that this was about the James case.

The sergeant stopped him as soon as he heard the name. "That was an OD," the cop told him.

"No," Alex replied, "it wasn't. Listen to this." One more time, he pressed the play icon on his smart phone.

Once again, the confrontation with Spencer played out. When it was done, the sergeant told the patrolman to put the bastard under arrest. "Read him his rights, Connors. Not that they'll do him any good."

The sergeant turned back to Alex and demanded his phone, which he willingly handed over. "The password is *Killer*, with a capital K. And would you please send a unit over to Rosie's to pick up his partner? She's being held by my girlfriend down in the dancer's dressing room. She goes by Sparkle, but her real name is Nancy Dawson:, skinny, twenties. Oh, and she's a meth addict."

The cop went back to looking pissed-off. "I'll do that, and I'll take her in along with both of you. How many laws did you break to accomplish your little heroics?"

"We may have bent a few, but I don't think we broke any. I never held

Spencer against his will, and my girlfriend has Dawson under citizen's arrest for meth possession. You'll be able to at least hold her on that."

"So you're mixed up in this too?" the cop asked Jake.

"Some," Jake agreed. "I think you're going to want to hear my side of this business."

Alex's phone went off at that moment, playing Bob Seeger's "Main Street" as a ring tone. "You'd better answer that," Alex told the cop. "If you don't, you're going to have one ticked-off dancer slash criminologist storming the place, and you may lose your other culprit."

The cop pushed the answer button and said, "Sergeant Riley, Waterford PD." Even without the speakerphone on, Alex could hear Charlie's voice demanding to know what the hell was happening.

"Mr. Strong is fine, miss. I'll send a couple of cars to pick up you and your prisoner. ID yourself to the officers when they arrive. Excuse me. I have work to do." He hung up.

"I ought to cuff both of you, but damned if I know what for right now. You *will* come down to the station with me. Any trouble and I *will* find something to hold you on. Material witnesses if nothing else."

The sergeant broke off to work his radio, telling dispatch to send two units to Rosie's and what they should expect when they got there.

"If you two heroes are ready, let's hit the road. You come with me. Connors, get that guy loaded up. Captain, if you'll excuse us, we'll get out of here and let you get back to work."

The ride to the police station was made in silence. When they got there, Alex and Jake were split up and stuck into interview rooms. Alex thought he heard Charlie's noisy arrival through the soundproofing, but he couldn't be sure.

After half an hour, Detective Samms entered the room. He made Alex repeat his story twice, comparing it with notes he'd obviously taken earlier. He was obviously pissed-off at getting called out at this time of night, but he didn't take it out on Alex … much.

He finally asked, "You never considered calling us with this new information, Mr. Strong?"

Alex shrugged and answered, "The case had been closed. We still didn't have any proof that Spencer was even in the plant until today. Now you can check the radiation checkpoint logs and see he was in the plant the night Walker died. A search of his phone will probably have an app to open the re-rack building doors."

Samms looked at Alex with a glare not much less menacing that the one Spencer had given him a couple of hours earlier. "I've spoken with Mr. Campbell," he told Alex. "I'll be back to see you when I'm done interviewing your other accomplice. Remain here." And with that, he left Alex alone again.

It was another hour before the door opened again and a parade of persons entered. The first one through the door was Charlie. She saw Alex and ran to him, almost knocking him over as he stood up. She hugged him hard, put her lips against his ear, and said, "You bastard. He was ready to kill you! Don't ever put me, or you, into a spot like that again!"

While she was speaking, the rest of the group filed in, including Detective Samms, Jake, and, bringing up the rear, Special Agent Harkness of the FBI.

Samms told everybody to sit down. Then he proceeded to rake them over the coals for getting involved in a homicide investigation. Alex wisely didn't interrupt to tell him that the ME had ruled out murder and the case was closed. Once he finished his chewing out, he went on in a milder tone.

"However, it appears you have corrected a miscarriage of justice. We have confessions from both Spencer and Nancy Dawson. We also discovered some additional information that you may find interesting. Agent Harkness?"

All eyes went to the FBI man. "The one thing you weren't sure about was how the money was getting diverted. I take it you're familiar with a man named Kevin Drummond?"

Alex's felt his eyes go wide and he couldn't help exclaim, "Drummond is in on this? How?"

Harkness held up his hand and continued. "I'll take that as a yes. It turns out that Drummond was the person diverting money from Trippler. There were two reasons we couldn't find the money trail. First, we were looking for money being diverted from Yankee Power, not from Trippler. Second, the money wasn't going into Spencer's pockets, it was going into accounts held by his girlfriend, Nancy Dawson. That's why Spencer's finances came up clean.

"You were correct in your assumption that Spencer was purposely screwing up that one project in order to increase the money going into his pocket. Mr. James must have figured it out and confronted Spencer. Spencer, with Ms. Dawson's help, killed him. He restrained him while Ms. Dawson used a bulb syringe to squirt meth up his nose."

"But how does Drummond fit in?" Alex demanded.

"Patience, Mr. Strong. Drummond is responsible for something called, if I recall correctly, the 'consolidated manpower and cost-summary report.'"

Alex's jaw dropped. "Drummond wrote that report. What has that got to do with it?"

Harkness continued. "Periodically, Drummond would run a modified version of the report that would change how charges to various projects, including the re-rack project, were apportioned. I believe there were multiple times that report failed and you didn't get the results as expected."

Alex could only nod yes.

"Those were the runs that were sweeping money into Ms. Dawson's accounts. Exotic dancers are actually employed as independent contractors. Did you know that? She had a shell identity set up, made to order to accept corporate deposits."

Alex looked at Jake and Charlie, struck dumb by the revelations they'd just heard.

"Spencer has rolled over on Drummond," Harkness continued. "Agents are en route to his home right now to take him into custody on fraud and racketeering charges. Spencer says that Drummond was not involved in the murder, so I doubt we can get him for conspiracy on that count."

Samms took over the narrative. "So the state will prosecute Spencer and Dawson for murder. The assistant US attorney will be seeking indictments against Drummond and Spencer for the RICO crimes Agent Harkness mentioned. All told, they're all going away for a long time. Thank you, all. You're free to go for now. I'm sure the state's attorney and the AUSA will be in touch. The desk sergeant will provide you with a ride."

Agent Harkness added, "Mr. Strong, Mr. Campbell, Ms. Edwards, thank you for your help. He turned his attention to Charlie. "Ms. Edwards,

I understand you are about to graduate from the forensics program at Conn College. Give me a call when you're out of school and I'll give you a recommendation to the FBI intern program. The bureau can use resourceful young women like you on our team."

Charlie's shocked expression gave way to a happy smile. "Thank you, sir. I'll do that. Thank you very much!"

"My pleasure. As Detective Samms said, you're all free to go."

Alex, Charlie, and Jake exchanged looks and then Jake said, "Where to now, folks?"

Alex responded, "My place. It's just down the road. We can get a cab later to pick up our cars. We need a break first."

Chapter 21

In fifteen minutes, they were at Alex's apartment. The three didn't speak much until they were inside. Alex's first act was to formally introduce Jake and Charlie. When Charlie offered her hand, Jake swept her up in one of his famous bear hugs. "Damn, it's good to finally meet you. You are even prettier than Alex told me."

Alex's next act was to ask, "Who wants a drink? Jake, you left a bottle of scotch here months ago. *Ms. Edwards,* I have bourbon and rum. Will either of those do? And how come I have to solve a murder to find out your real name? What's your first name, anyway?"

Charlie gave him a punch on the shoulder and said, "It's Charlene, okay? Now you know. And yes, it did take a murder, and if you have some Coke to go with the rum, I'll take it."

Alex let Jake mix his own scotch while he got one for Charlie (*It'll take a long time to break that habit!*) and bourbon for himself. When they were all settled in the living room, they quietly sipped their drinks.

After a while, Jake broke the silence. "Old man, you pretty well had your ass in a sling there. You're one lucky guy."

Alex shook his head and replied, "No, not with Charlene backing me up. Her timing was perfect. Honey, how did you corner Sparkle or Nancy or whatever her name is?"

"It wasn't hard. I told her I wanted to make a little deal and she took me right downstairs. Tanya kept everybody else out while we finished our business. You should send her some flowers."

"I will. What can I do for you?" Alex asked her.

"You can get me another drink to start with," she told him.

"Will do. Jake?"

"Not me. I need to head for home and get some sleep before facing the music from management tomorrow. I actually ordered a cab while you were mixing drinks. It'll be here any minute. There's an app for that, you know."

His feeble attempt at humor put the other two into hysterics, and after a few seconds, he couldn't help himself and joined in. Only the sound of the cab blowing its horn out front killed the laughter and tears.

Jake and Alex swapped hugs, Jake kissed Charlene on the cheek, and then he grabbed his coat and headed out the door, leaving Charlene and Alex alone.

As soon as the door was closed, Charlene was in Alex's arms. Her head was on his chest and she was crying again, not hysterical tears but tears of fear. "I was sure that bastard was going to kill you! Why'd I ever agree to go along with that crazy scheme of yours?"

Alex gently lifted her chin up and kissed away her tears. "I'm fine, we're all fine, and the bad guys are in jail. I'm never going to be involved in anything like this again. But *you* are going to be a star FBI agent. How about that?"

Charlene started crying again, stammering something about not wanting to ever see him again and not wanting to move to Virginia, all the words jumbled up. Her last words, evidently the answer to his question about being a star FBI agent, were "Pretty damn cool."

Alex kissed away her tears again and said, "You know, it only takes about three hours to get to Virginia in the Cardinal. It's not that long a trip. And who knows? Maybe I can find a job near Quantico. Lots of contracting work in the district."

"You'd better," she told him. "You'd better be down there every weekend. Alex, I thought this was just the excitement of my first murder investigation, but it's more than that. Do you feel it too?"

"Yeah, honey, I do. What are we going to do about it?"

"Well, the first thing we're going to do is get back in that weird bed of yours. And this time, we're not just going to fall asleep!"

That was logic Alex couldn't fault.

Author's Notes

I'm sure that careful readers familiar with the New London/Waterford area of southeastern Connecticut will find exception to a number of details in this story. Allow me to try to set your minds at ease.

Osprey Point is obviously based on the Millstone Point generating facility. The name came to me because of the many ospreys I saw while biking back and forth to work via the old Millstone Road. It never was the largest nuclear generating station in the world but did rank very high when all three units were operating. I have no factual knowledge of any of the plant's security systems, only what I observed while working there in the 1980s. All else is deduction, supposition, and literary license.

The Sunset Ribs Co. is an actual restaurant. Pete is pure fiction.

There is a Roses Cantina located in Groton, Connecticut. Since it is just up the road from the submarine base, it is loaded with memorabilia donated by members of the "Silent Service". There is no Rosie's in Waterford and never has been. Its fictional location is occupied by The Dock Restaurant.

Waterford Airport was a privately owned, public-use airport just off I-95. Unfortunately, it closed in the 1980s due to pressure from residents who bought the homes next to the airport with dreams of developing the property. The proposed development fell through, and the great irony is that the homes were originally built by people who had airplanes based at the airport. Go figure.

The author gratefully acknowledges Paul Freeman and his Web site Abandoned and Little Known Airports for information on Waterford airport.

The airplane is also real. I've been a partner in a Cessna Cardinal since 1998. It only seemed right to give it a role in solving this mystery. It has an even bigger role in the next book, already in progress.

D.S.R, Holden, Mass.

www.ingramcontent.com/pod-product-compliance
Lightning Source LLC
Chambersburg PA
CBHW051842170626
46807CB00003B/1306